AARZU ALL AROUND

MARZIEH ABBAS

SALAAM READS

NEW YORK   AMSTERDAM/ANTWERP   LONDON   TORONTO
SYDNEY/MELBOURNE   NEW DELHI

For all the hijabis.
May our stories be celebrated, our voices heard,
and our dreams realized.
Ameen.

An imprint of Simon & Schuster Children's Publishing Division
1230 Avenue of the Americas, New York, New York 10020
For more than 100 years, Simon & Schuster has championed authors and the stories they create. By respecting the copyright of an author's intellectual property, you enable Simon & Schuster and the author to continue publishing exceptional books for years to come. We thank you for supporting the author's copyright by purchasing an authorized edition of this book.
No amount of this book may be reproduced or stored in any format, nor may it be uploaded to any website, database, language-learning model, or other repository, retrieval, or artificial intelligence system without express permission. All rights reserved. Inquiries may be directed to Simon & Schuster, 1230 Avenue of the Americas, New York, NY 10020 or permissions@simonandschuster.com.
This book is a work of fiction. Any references to historical events, real people, or real places are used fictitiously. Other names, characters, places, and events are products of the author's imagination, and any resemblance to actual events or places or persons, living or dead, is entirely coincidental.
Text © 2025 by Marzieh Abbas
Jacket illustration © 2025 by Chaaya Prabhat
Jacket design by Laura Eckes
All rights reserved, including the right of reproduction in whole or in part in any form.
SALAAM READS and its logo are trademarks of Simon & Schuster, LLC.
For information about special discounts for bulk purchases, please contact Simon & Schuster Special Sales at 1-866-506-1949 or business@simonandschuster.com.
Simon & Schuster strongly believes in freedom of expression and stands against censorship in all its forms. For more information, visit BooksBelong.com.
The Simon & Schuster Speakers Bureau can bring authors to your live event. For more information or to book an event, contact the Simon & Schuster Speakers Bureau at 1-866-248-3049 or visit our website at www.simonspeakers.com.
Interior design by Laura Eckes
The text for this book was set in Perpetua.
The illustrations for this book were rendered in ink.
Manufactured in the United States of America
First Edition
2 4 6 8 10 9 7 5 3 1
CIP data for this book is available from the Library of Congress.
ISBN 9781665970419
ISBN 9781665970433 (ebook)

Also by Marzieh Abbas

A Dupatta Is . . .
ABC's of Pakistan
Henna Is . . .
Awe-Samosas!
A Ramadan to Remember
Yasmeen Lari, Green Architect
The Camel Library

Nadia and Nadir
Visit Pakistan
Ramadan Cookies
Eid Surprises
Beach-Trash Art
Hurricane Helpers
Lunch in the Leaves
Architect Assistants
Backyard Mystery
Compost Scraps
Host and Hostess
Run for a Cause
Slime Time

Hamza's Pyjama Promise
Hamza and Aliya Share the Ramadan Cheer
Hamza and Aliya Share a Surprise

Excited for Eid
Friday Fun
Day by Day

CRICKET VOCABULARY

BOUNCER: a short-pitched delivery that bounces once on the pitch and reaches the batswoman/batsman at head height, usually meant to take a player by surprise and force them onto their back foot so they play a defensive, rather than an attacking, shot

BOUNDARY: the rope around the edge of the cricket field; a ball that is hit hard enough to cross the rope is also called a boundary

CORK BALL: a ball made of cork and covered with leather, used on hard pitches in games such as cricket

DOT-BALL: a ball (bowled by the bowler) from which no runs are scored (by the batswoman/batsman)

FIELD SETTING: the way the fielding/bowling team positions their players; this involves strategy and planning

GOLDEN DUCK: when the batswoman/batsman is out on the first ball

MAIDEN: when the bowler delivers an entire over without the batswoman/batsman managing to score a run

OVER: a set of six legal deliveries bowled by a bowler to the batswomen/batsmen on the opposing team

PITCH: A cricket pitch consists of the central strip of the grassy cricket field that lies between the wickets. It is twenty-two yards long and ten feet wide. The surface is flat and is normally covered with extremely short grass but can be completely dry with dusty soil. The batswomen/batsmen take their places at either end of the pitch.

PROTECTIVE GEAR (also called pads/guards): guards worn by batswomen/batsmen to protect themselves from the impact of a ball hitting them

SIXER: six runs scored when the batswoman/batsman hits the ball directly over the boundary

WICKET: a structure made of three long, vertical sticks (called stumps) that balance two short, horizontal sticks (called bails). Each end of the cricket pitch is fitted with a wicket. Wickets also refer to the number of batswomen/batsmen dismissed, as in "taking wickets" or "losing wickets"

WIDE: a kind of extra ball where the bowler bowls too far off for the batswoman/batman's bat to make contact with the ball

YORKER: a ball pitched at the bottom of a batswoman/batsman's bat, making it difficult for them to execute a shot

BASIC RULES OF CRICKET

CRICKET IS A BAT-AND-BALL GAME PLAYED BETWEEN TWO teams. It is played on a circular or oval grass field with a rectangular area at the center called the pitch. The pitch is a hardened, smooth surface that is twenty-two yards long and ten feet wide. It is where most of the action, including batting and bowling, occurs.

Each end of the pitch has a structure called a wicket. Each wicket is made of three long, vertical sticks (called stumps) that balance two short, horizontal sticks (called bails).

Each team consists of eleven active players. Spare players join the active squad if an active player gets injured.

Games are composed of sides take turns at batting and bowling (pitching); each turn is called an "innings" (always plural).

The fielding team will have a bowler bowl (pitch) the ball to the batswoman/batsman, who tries to hit the ball with their bat.

A bowler bowls (or delivers) six balls to complete an over. The next over is bowled by another bowler on the same team.

The fielding/bowling team tries to get the batswoman/batsman out by . . .

- hitting the wickets with the ball when bowling,
- catching a batswoman's/batsman's shot before the ball touches the ground,
- hitting the batswoman's/batsman's leg with the ball in

front of the wicket (LBW, or leg before wicket), or
- hitting the wickets with the ball before the batsmen can run to the other end of the pitch (run out).

Each time the batswoman/batsman runs one full length of the pitch, it equals one run. The players try to score as many runs as possible before getting out, by . . .

- hitting the ball, running between the wickets, and making it to the other end before the fielders can hit the wickets with the ball,
- hitting the ball to the boundary along the ground, which equals four runs, or
- hitting the ball directly over the boundary, which equals six runs.

The fielding team must get ten batswomen/batsmen out before they can switch places and start batting.

Extras are the runs scored by methods other than striking the ball with the bat. An extra scored by, or awarded to, a batting team is not credited to any individual batswoman/batsman. There are five types of extras: no balls, wides, byes, leg byes, and penalty runs.

The aim of the game is to score as many runs as possible. The team with the most runs wins.

Learn more about the laws of cricket here: lords.org/mcc/the-laws-of-cricket

Match Day

The final match of the
international Cricket World Cup
is today.
My team, Pakistan,
plays the defending champions, Australia.
Match Day is always a good day—
unless Pakistan loses.
In which case
Match Day is the worst day.

We peer down

onto the dirt road
from our third-floor balcony.
The slums of Karachi are
PuLsInG
with a carnival-like atmosphere—
a sea of white and emerald green,
the color of Pakistan's flag.

The aroma of freshly fried samosas wafts up
from a kiosk at the entrance to our building,
along with a whiff of
cardamom-flavored,
sugar-drenched jalebis;
crispy-on-the-outside,
chewy-on-the-inside.
Boys with melty kulfi sticks in hand
line up like dominoes
snaking around the narrow lane,
continuing around the curb,
to get their faces painted green
for a rupee each.
Occasionally one pushes another
and they *topple*

                    topple

                              topple

                                      over

                                              one another,
                  making my sister, Sukoon, and me laugh.

Upstairs

I balance my new cricket journal
in one hand,
with Sukoon's lab reports
carefully sandwiched between its pages.
I clench a pen firmly between my teeth
and leave one hand free,
to alternate between

                        parting the leaves obscuring my view,
cheering for our team,
                  and swatting the flies that irritate my face.
Sukoon and I
keep our heads low,
just in case Khaloo glances up.
If he catches a glimpse of us,
our uncle will come home nagging
about how girls shouldn't be seen
on their balconies
and what girls should
and shouldn't be doing. . . .

Pitching In

My cousins, Irfan and Arsal,
have pitched in
a total of sixty-five rupees,
along with their friends
from our neighborhood,
for the projector
and loudspeaker rental
that have been hoisted up in our lane for Match Day.
I know because I helped them
count their money . . .
my way, the smart way.

Smart

I made my younger cousin, Irfan, arrange his coins
in stacks of five.
(That's how old he and my sister, Sukoon, are.)
It's also the highest number
Irfan can write and count to

in both English and Urdu.
His coins made thirteen stacks.
(That's how old I am going to turn.)
Then I made Arsal
count by fives.
I'm glad he remembered
the five times table
I've been teaching him
for the last month.
One stack—five coins,
two stacks—ten coins,
. . . fifteen, twenty, twenty-five . . .
all the way up to sixty-five!
This quick calculation
made Irfan swoon and say,
Aaru Aappi, you're soooooo smart!
But Arsal just rolled his eyes
because never in a million years
would he have thought
of counting
my way . . .
the smart way.

Not Smart

My uncle, Khaloo, their father, didn't think
his sons were being smart when they gave away
all that money for the screen rental.
SIXTY RUPEES?
His voice boomed as
he crossed his arms firmly over his broad chest,
side-eyeing his wife, our aunt, Khala Ammi.
His up-curled mustache twitched in disapproval.
We could've bought
a pound of potatoes and just enough onions
for your mother to make sabzi,
with sixty rupees. . . .

Sixty-five, Baba.
It was five more than . . .
Arsal's voice
t r a i l e d

when Khaloo stared him
D
O
W
N.

But I could tell
from Khaloo's not-so-angry voice
when he spoke about the trade-offs
that he was just as excited
as his sons
about watching the match
on this special makeshift screen
in the company of friends and neighbors.

Allowed

The boys are allowed
to join the men
in the neighborhood chai café
to watch the match
on a makeshift screen
projected against
a whitewashed wall.
The cheering crowd
thickens downstairs.
I spot my cousins,
Arsal and Irfan,

their names glistening

on their deep emerald jerseys,

just like the uniform

the international players wear.

I wish I had a jersey

with my name,

Aarzu Raza, in glittery gold.

My eyes linger on the boys

sharing a green Pakola soda,

huddled together,

rooting for our team,

on a woven charpoy with friends.

I long for the day

when I can do the same. . . .

Not Allowed

I wish we still had a TV at home

on which we could watch the match,

but Khala Ammi says Khaloo refused

to buy another after Irfan,

as a toddler,

smashed theirs to pieces

while reaching for a toy
placed above the TV.
My knees grow sore
from crouching
between the purple periwinkle
and magenta bougainvillea
clay pots lining the balcony.
But I don't want to miss
even a minute of the entertainment.
Sukoon joins me on the balcony.
It is a rare day when her body isn't swollen
or she isn't burning in fever.
Her ailing kidney
must be doing okay today, I guess.
She fits into the space between
the white jasmine and orange marigold pots.
She's holding her crescent-and-star flag
that we painted together
and stuck to a used straw.
Every time Pakistani players take a wicket
during Pakistan's bowling innings
and every time a Pakistani batsman
scores a boundary
during Pakistan's batting innings,
Sukoon waves her straw flag.

Khaloo thinks

girls should

be in the kitchen.

serve the men and boys of the household.

study in public, all-girls schools if they must study at all.

train young to be housewives.

girls shouldn't

be on their balconies.

eat until after the men and boys have eaten.

study beyond grade ten.

play outdoors. (Oh, how my hands twitch to hold a cricket bat in an open cricket field, or even downstairs in our lane, where Arsal goes to play.)

Baba

Thankfully, all men are not like Khaloo.
My baba was the opposite of him.
He was fearless and caring.
The earth s
         w
            a
              l
               l
                o
                 w
                  e
                    d Mama and Baba whole,
and their bodies were never recovered
from the heaps of rubble
the earthquake left behind.
I am happy they
have each other
and am glad Sukoon and I
have each other
and the best memories with them.

Baba used to say
Prophet Muhammad (peace be upon him)
stood up in respect
for his daughter Fatimah (peace be upon her).
Baba did the same for us girls.
You are my flowers,
not just my daughters. . . .
I want to see you bloom, he'd say.

Baba was a cricket player
(one of the best on the Pakistani team)
and dreamt we girls
would also play cricket someday.
There's nothing you can't do, he'd assure us,
as long as you find a way to do it!

Mama's Fondest Memory

Mama always smiled
when she recalled the time
Baba bought me a plastic cricket bat and ball
from a roadside thella.

He ripped off the packaging,
knelt on the ground,
placed me on my pudgy baby feet,
and held my sagging diaper sides,
steadying me.
Mama would
laugh out loud
when she got to this bit:
*She can barely stand,
I'd told him . . .*
but Baba was adamant.
He repeated the words *bismillah, bismillah*
and made me take my first steps
toward the cricket bat and ball
that he balanced in his lap.
He stretched his hands forward
on either side of me
to catch me if I fell.

Mama

My mama was a teacher,
a literature teacher.
The verses of Iqbal and Faiz,
Rumi, Mir and Ghalib,
flowed from her lips
like the water that gushed
from the mountains that surrounded our home.
Since Mama was
one of few women who taught
in our village at the foot of the mountains,
the whole of our small town
called her *Teacher Aunty*,
a title that made her cheeks blush rosy pink.

She taught me so much,
but no amount of knowledge
will ever add up
to what Arsal and Irfan have
just being born
boys.

Keeping Score

Arsal, my cousin, is a mini version of his dad, my khaloo.
And because Arsal is the same age as me,
I keep score with him
like in a cricket tournament.

Tournament Scoreboard

	Aarzu	Arsal
Academic achievement	1	0
Long lashes	0	1
Sucking up to Khaloo	0	1
Veg-chopping skills	1	0
Helping Khala Ammi	1	0
Athletic ability	1	0
Responsible	1	0

I'm better at most stuff.
But because Arsal is a boy,
it makes no difference
       that I am more athletic,
       that I am smarter at schoolwork,

        that I am better at housework,
        that I am more helpful to Khala Ammi;
no virtue is good enough.
Nothing else matters.
In Khaloo's house,
being a boy
gives him a million points >>against<< any girl!

Cricket Journal

During commercial breaks,
when the clamor and clanking of soda cans
and plastic water bottles
fill the space
between the overs,
I flip to the first page
of the new journal
my new best friend, Nazia, gifted me,
and doodle a border
of cricket bats, cork balls, and wickets.
With thirteen runs required off six balls by Pakistan,
I work out the possibilities to victory—

a necessary skill for a future cricket player.
The journal is divided into two halves
by a single
separator.
I wonder what I will use
the second half for.

Interruptions

Aar-zuuuuuuuuu!
Su-koooooooooon!
Jaldi aao, jaldi aao,
time to make the rotis,
Khala Ammi yells
loud enough
for the entire five floors
of our building to hear.
Khaloo and the boys will be home soon.
Cut the lemons.
Pluck the coriander.
Lay the table!
I bite my lip,

bring myself to my feet,
scratch the back of my left leg
with the tip of my right foot,
and blink away tears.

Timing

Perfect timing, Khalajaan!
I jab the lid back onto my pen.
Snap my journal shut.
The commentator's pitch rises to a shriek.
Ten runs required off five balls.
Khan, Pakistan's current best batsman
[and Baba's ex-teammate],
steals three runs
where there seemed to be only a double.
Aaaaand, he scrapes through,
just making his ground . . .
barely avoiding a run out.
The crowd cheers and chants his nickname.
BOOM-BOOM, BOOM-BOOM.
I glance back one last time

to blow a prayer toward our players.
Sukoon, already inside the house,
furrows her brows,
tugs at the end of my kurta,
urging me to hurry inside
as if *she* is the older sister.

I want to tell Khala Ammi

        it is the last over of the match.
I want to tell Khala Ammi
        my favorite player,
        Baba's best friend,
        Uncle Baseer Khan,
        is the striker.
I want to tell Khala Ammi
        I need to do my part for Pakistan;
        blow   b l o w   b l o w
        prayers to the players
        like Mama used to
        toward the TV screen,
        toward Baba

       when he played for Pakistan.
I want to tell Khala Ammi
       I hate making rotis.
I want to tell Khala Ammi
       I hate crouching
       into invisibility.
I want to tell Khala Ammi
       I miss my baba,
       who'd haul Sukoon up onto his shoulders
       and carry me on his hip
       for a better view
       when he took us to watch
       matches at the stadium.
I want to tell Khala Ammi
       it could've been my baba
       batting right now
       (the expert pinch hitter
       always pulled up the order
       when quick runs were needed),
       if he hadn't died
       in that fateful earthquake.
I want to tell Khala Ammi
       we can buy the rotis
       from the tandoor wala in our lane.

I scratch the back of my left leg
with the tip of my right foot.
The only words I whisper are:
I wish I were a boy!

Kitchen Fun?

Even though my whisper is soft,
softer than the crackle of curry leaves in the pan,
Khala Ammi hears me and gives me her
you-didn't-really-mean-to-say-that look.
The aroma of perfectly stewed korma
swirls up our nostrils.
I savor it, letting it fill my insides
with a deep belly-breath.
Beads of sweat, the size of sesame seeds,
dot Khala Ammi's forehead and nose.
Larger sweat beads,
the size of coriander seeds,
speckle her upper lip.
When the beads grow close,
they join together into rivulets

and trickle down her neck.
Khala Ammi wipes them away
with the edge of her cotton dupatta.
She playfully dodges, jabs her rolling pin into my arm,
before blowing me a kiss
off her flour-dusted palm.
A puff of white lands on my cheek.
She blows another puff of white
to Sukoon as she hands her
a bunch of fresh coriander stalks
to pluck for the korma garnish.
Khala Ammi's single dimple
plays hide-and-seek on her left cheek,
just like Mama's. . . .
It makes me want to forget
about the match,
drop the rolling pin,
cup her face in my palms, and stare at her.
Khala Ammi has already made rotis,
perfect fluffy discs of flatbread,
for Khaloo and the boys.
Now it is my turn
to practice my dreaded roti-making skills

(not that I ever want to perfect such an art)
on rotis that Khala Ammi, Sukoon, and I will eat,
no matter what shape they turn out to be.

Pressure

Fleming bowls a wide,
a delivery bowled too far out
for the batsman to reach with his bat.
An extra run is awarded to Pakistan,
and the ball doesn't even count!
Oh, that's a fast one!
It's beat the wicketkeeper's gloves.
It's racing away to the boundary . . .
five free runs to Pakistan!
Pressure! Pressure!
I imagine Fleming, the Australian bowler,
wincing at his folly—
these extras could cost his team the match
and the tournament.
I lurch up and punch the air with the rolling pin.
A pot and two sieves

hanging from nails
that jut out above the kitchen counter
come clanking down onto me.
I roll my torso into a ball
to shield myself from the falling utensils.
Sukoon giggles and says,
Aapi, you look funny!
Sukoon's giggles are so rare,
with all her health problems,
that I do a slow-motion repeat
of the sieves falling on me,
with exaggerated facial expressions,
just to hear her laugh again.

Aaru!

Aaru!
Khala Ammi pitches her voice high.
Arms akimbo,
she pretends to be upset
with my clumsiness in the kitchen.
But her lips twitch
before curling at the corners.

Her dimple sneaks up
to her left cheek
as she too bursts into laughter.
I love it when she calls me *Aaru*—
it literally translates to "peaches," and
it's the name my parents called me.

Match day food

is always special.
If Pakistan wins the match,
Khala Ammi says
the meal serves as a celebration.
If we lose (God forbid),
the food serves as a balm,
calming tense nerves.
So, no matter how simply we eat
all week long,
Match Day food
is never simple.
Sometimes it's biryani
(my favorite dish, and thankfully, Khaloo's too),
aromatic and flavorful

long grains of basmati rice
tinged golden with saffron,
layered with meat and potatoes: spicy and yum.
Sometimes it's dum ka keema,
smoked mincemeat
cooked in butter and ghee,
topped with green coriander leaves,
ginger sticks,
and a generous squeeze of lemon juice.
Today, whether
we win
or lose,
Khala Ammi's menu
is a winner.

A Winning Menu

Main course:

                                                Korma:
                ginger and garlic sautéed in hot ghee.
                        Onions fried deep golden.
                    Goat meat braised in yogurt
                      spiced with coriander, cumin,

turmeric, and red chili powder.
Slow cooked.
A sprinkling of garam masala:
ground cardamom pods, black peppercorns, cinnamon.
Garnished with ginger sticks,
coriander leaves, and love.

Side:

Baingan Raita:
eggplant, grilled.
Spiced with pink Himalayan salt.
Topped with yogurt.
Tempered with curry leaves and mustard seeds.

Drinks:

Lassi:
sweet and salty
yogurt whisked by hand.
Topped with a layer of thick cream
from a pot of freshly boiled buffalo milk.
Two cubes of ice top off each glass.

Dessert:

Shahi Tukray:
bread slices cut into triangles,
fried in ghee,
topped with sweet saffron milk,
sprinkled with cardamom.

Guilt

and hunger
gurgle inside me
when I see Khala Ammi's feast
bubbling in pots—
I wish I'd helped her out more
in the kitchen.

Totkas

Khala Ammi has remedies for
everything.
Just like the magic of Mama's hugs,
Khala Ammi's totkas can fix
all.

Bad throat?
Squeeze ginger juice into honey, sprinkle pepper. Gulp.
Voila, throat is fine!

Stuffy nose?

Cut an onion in half, leave by your bedside.
Get up with an unblocked nose!

Stained shirt?
Sprinkle talcum powder and dissolve in vinegar and soda water.
Boom! No stain.

Burnt hand?
Dip hand in egg white and cold flour.
No blisters!

Hard poop?
One tablespoon of castor oil. Swallow.
BLAST!

Today she has mistakenly added
a bit too much salt in the korma.
She asks me to drop a ball
of unsalted aata dough into the curry.
It'll suck up all the excess salt
as it sits in the simmering pot
without interfering with the flavor.

The casual tone of Khala Ammi's instructions
tells me this is a tried and tested totka.

I wish Khala Ammi had a tried and tested totka
that could suck up my guilt
for not helping her with meal prep,
while still allowing me to enjoy the match!

Final Tense Moments

I roll aata dough into a ball,
then flatten between my palms into a disc
before rolling it with my bailan for a roti.
My shaky hands and sweaty palms produce an
uneven-on-the-edges, elongated roti . . .
more the shape of Pakistan's map
than the perfectly circular
planet shape it should be.
Team Pakistan just needs
two runs from four balls, Khala Ammi!
I will optimism into my words.
But we only have one player left to bat, Aaru!
says Khala Ammi matter-of-factly.
BOOM! BOOM! turns to BOO! BOO!
Cheers change to jeers

telling us another wicket has

                        fallen.

Khan is **OUT**.

Khala Ammi bites her lip.

I scratch the back of my left shin

with the tip of my right foot

and smack my rolled roti onto the hot tawa.

Sukoon plucks the coriander leaves extra hard.

We're down to our last player.

If we lose the tournament after coming this close,

I doubt even Khala Ammi's food will soothe

our tense nerves.

But before I can flip my roti,

chanting from our lane,

ChhakKA, chhakKA,

reVERbeRATES

through my veins!

The new batsman on strike

has hit a SIX. . . .

Pakistan wins!

Victory songs

throb through us,
BOOM-BOOM, BOOM, BOOM,
loud enough to make our metal utensils rattle.
We run to the balcony,
me still clutching my rolling pin
and a fresh ball of aata dough,
Sukoon swaying coriander stalks instead of her straw flag,
and this time Khala Ammi runs out behind us.
She crouches between us near the potted plants.
Boys and men form circles in the narrow lanes.
Their hands are streamers above their heads
as they hop around to the beat of
patriotic-themed commercial ads.
Joy masks my senses as I watch the replay
of the sixer that won us the tournament.
I bounce into the air
from my squatting position
and instinctively toss my dough ball
while swinging my rolling pin,
more like a baseball bat
than a cricket bat. . . .

wHOOSH

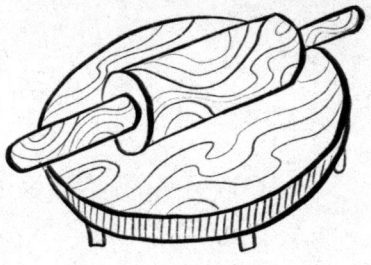

Out goes the dough ball
and out slips the rolling pin
from my floured hands.
Khala Ammi lunges
        over the railing
                and misses the dough ball
                        and almost misses the bailan
until . . . she doesn't!
AARU! she shrieks.
We burst into giggles.
Thankfully, the loudspeakers
blasting catchy songs are loud enough
so we too can sing along,
A L O U D!

Victory Dance

Sukoon, Khala, and I

move the sparse furniture

inside our two-bedroom apartment

to the side to make enough room

for us to line up beside each other.

We drape our dupattas

from our left shoulders,

cross body,

and knot them to the right of our hips.

We swish our hands up in the air

in a windshield-wiper motion,

form Vs with our fingers,

mimicking the victory song moves

that flash on the makeshift screen.

We dance, free and fearless

of Khaloo returning home

anytime soon.

The Best Day

And just like that
> Pakistan beats
> the defending champions,
> Australia.

And just like that
> Match Day is indeed
> a good day.
> Match Day is
> the best day,
> as sweet as the jaggery halva
> Baba used to bring home
> to celebrate
> Pakistan's every win.
> And just like that
> lunch today
> will indeed
> be a celebration!

After dancing

and having cut the lemons
and having set the table
and folding the laundry with Sukoon
and sorting the clothes into our cardboard boxes
and playing a game of ludo with Sukoon and Khala Ammi
      and waiting
      and waiting
      and waiting
for Khaloo and the boys to return,
I complete the first entry
in my cricket journal
while a tired Sukoon
rests her head on a pillow beside me.

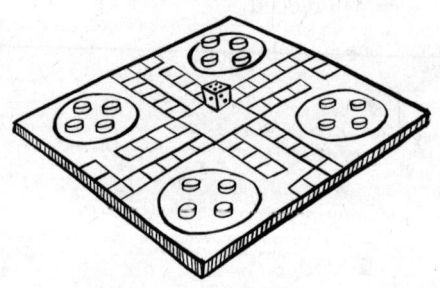

Cricket Journal Entry

International Cricket World Cup Final
Saturday, September 19th
Pakistan vs. Australia
Final score Pakistan: 224
Final score Australia: 219
Man of the Match: (Uncle) Baseer Khan
(for the highest runs scored)

Suddenly I know what I want to do with the second half of my new journal. . . .

Aarzu Raza's Journal

is what I label the divider.

I write *WISH*,

the meaning of my name, beneath.

As Sukoon nods off

for a nap on our shared mattress,

I write my first entry.

Aarzu

Mama chose my name.
It was from the title
of her favorite poem
by Pakistan's visionary poet
Allama Iqbal.

Mama's Lullaby

You,
you,
you are my Aarzu.
I truly hope
your every wish comes true!
(I hope so too, Mama!)

Sukoon

When Sukoon was going to be born,
MamaBaba thought long and hard about her name.
It'll make her personality, Baba said.
It'll be a prayer
inspiring the course of her life, Mama said.
Baba spoke to neighbors and friends.
Mama dug into poems, dictionaries, and religious texts.
We need balance in our family....
Mama is hardworking, always hustling.
Aarzu, you're driven, always wishing for more!
Baba said, planting a kiss on my forehead.
And, Baba, you're successful, always breaking records! I added.
Baba beamed, and then blushed.
We need stillness, Mama said,
someone who is at peace
and brings peace to others.
I've always liked the name Sakeena,
from the Arabic root letters sa-ka-na,
meaning "rest, peace, tranquility."
The discussion continued for months.
I remember it so clearly.

Similar names
with the same meaning
were repeated—
Sukaynah, Sakeena, Sukoon, Taskeen—
to see which rolled off our tongues.
One day after evening reading time with Mama,
I declared,
Sukoon! We'll call her Sukoon!
The long oo sound is like a baby cooing,
and my sister will be the cutest cooing baby EVER!
It was decided.
Now, as I look at Sukoon
living with a kidney condition,
easily tired, at times feverish, mostly in pain,
I feel no peace and no tranquility.
Only an aarzu, a wish, a longing, for my parents,
who are no more, to help us figure this out.

Green

Green...
the Pakistan team jersey

sporting a crescent and star.

Green...
the dupatta I wear
to blend in with the plants
on Khala Ammi's balcony.

Green...
Arsal's hand-me-*up* jersey
like the Pakistan cricket team's
jersey from last year
that I wear under my kurta
to cheer for my team.

Green...
the parrots perched
on the electric poles
free to flap and fly.

Green...
the envy
that simmers within me
wishing I'd been born a boy...
born free to play for Pakistan, like Baba.

Forbidden Treasure

Khaloo and the boys return home
an hour after the match has ended,
while celebration bells still ring in the streets.
Irfan tiptoes into our shared bedroom
as I am redoing my coconut-oiled hair
into a tight braid.
He gently shuts the door
with a flick of his hip,
imitating a Bollywood actress's thumka dance
in an attempt to make me laugh,
his life mission!
He commands me to shut my eyes.
No peeking, Aaru Aapi! he warns.
He flips my hands over,
places something warm and crumbly
into my palms.
Closes my fingers
around the mush.
One, two, three, four—

                                    Can I see now?

I interrupt.

. . . nine, ten.

He stretches every second

to add to the suspense.

Open, open, Aaru Aapi!

I open my eyes and fingers

to expose a warm, corners-nibbled,

almost-squashed samosa

in my palms.

Eat it fast, Aaru Aapi!

Before Arsal or Abu see.

His eyes twinkle

a combination of mischief and pride.

Any sewage water on this? I tease.

Irfan has fallen into open manholes

that dot the dirt roads of our slum

at least six times in the twelve months

Sukoon and I have been living with Khala Ammi's family.

He cocks his collar up,

juts his chest out,

holds one elbow forward like a shield.

Aaru Aapi, he says, bowing his head,

mimicking a knight,

your samosa is too precious.

I'd guard it with my life!

Between hushed giggles
I signal to him to wake Sukoon.
I inspect the remains of the squished samosa
as if eyeing a retrieved treasure.
Khaloo would never approve of his son
spending money
to smuggle street food
for Sukoon and me.
The samosa smells of victory.
When Irfan holds out sleepy Sukoon's palm,
I split the oozing potato-filled samosa into two.
I hand the bigger half to Sukoon,
purse my lips together, squeeze my eyes shut,
and blow Irfan a kiss of gratitude.
The flaky crust is soggy
from the time it has spent
in Irfan's pocket.
I pop my half
of smuggled samosa
into my mouth:
garam masala, crushed cumin, and coriander
EXPLODE.
I s l o w l y roll the bite back and forth,
forth and back,

left to right,

right to left,

savoring

every

morsel,

only allowing it to slip

d

o

w

n

my throat

as Khala Ammi

calls us to hurry out.

Price for a Treasure

Sorry, Aappi, I couldn't get the sweet jalebi for you.
They were too sticky to carry in my pocket, says Irfan.
I was scared Abu would've noticed the syrup drip.
I wince at the thought of the oil stain
the samosa must've left on Irfan's kameez pocket.
I make a mental note to soak it

in soapy water right after lunch
so it will be easy to scrub off
when I wash the clothes on Monday morning.
I trap his head with one hand
and rub the knuckles of my other hand
against his scraggly hair.
He squirms away,
spins around on his way out of the room,
and winks at us, one finger on his lips,
reminding us to keep
this secret.

Totka Success

Khala Ammi's totka has worked!
The korma is perfectly seasoned.
While Khaloo and the boys eat,
Khala Ammi busies herself
making a special masala chai:
cardamom, cinnamon, and cloves
brewed in sweet milk tea.
Sukoon and I

lay out Khala Ammi's special tea set,

the hand-painted one

that Khala Ammi usually only uses for Eid.

'Cause in this household,

like many others in Pakistan,

cricket is a religion,

and victory calls for celebration!

Khaloo pats his tummy

and lets out a loud,

unapologetic burp,

his way of excusing himself

from the table and maybe even appreciating the meal.

Khala Ammi sets out the shahi tukray and chai.

Sukoon and I

bring out our box of

oblong rotis, now cold,

and wait for Khala Ammi to join us

to eat the most delicious meal

of tender meat

falling off the bone.

We smack our lips

and lick our fingers

and the last smidge of

flavorful stew

off the korma curry bowl.

Air-Conditioning

The mid-September temperatures
have passed a hundred and five today.
Surprisingly, the government hasn't switched off
our electricity
for scheduled load-shedding.
(They're possibly too distracted by Pakistan's win.)
After we're done with lunch,
Khaloo switches on
the air-conditioning in his room,
the only room in the house with an air conditioner.
(Even though it's secondhand, it is a luxury.)
Khala Ammi gets her embroidery threads,
needles, and cloth,
and sinks into her rocking chair
with a cup of chai.
Arsal, Irfan, Sukoon, and I
collect the carom board,
discs, and powder,
shut the door behind us,
and settle into a corner of Khala Ammi and Khaloo's cool room
for a lazy afternoon.

Cooling Down

When all of us
and especially Khaloo cool off,
our spirits still high from Pakistan's win,
and Khala Ammi has brought him
another hand-painted cup
of steaming masala chai,
she signals to me
with a tilt of her head
(ever so slight)
and a flick of her eyes.

Khala Ammi and I are like cricket players
on the same team
building a partnership,
understanding each other's slightest gestures,
executing a strategy
we're both in on.

It is time
to share Sukoon's reports
with Khaloo—

to ask him to help fund her treatment:
medication, tests, and doctor's charges.

We hope Khaloo will agree,
despite meager earnings from driving his rickshaw,
to shell out some money
to save Sukoon's life.

I Have an Extra

When we visited the doctor
last week,
he explained it to us like this:
Some organs
you have extras of—
two eyes,
two lungs,
two kidneys—

and some you don't . . .
one liver,
one heart,

one brain.

But my sister,
my only sister,
Sukoon,
was born
short of one kidney.

It normally isn't an issue,
the doctor explained,
except Sukoon's facing
some complications
[a big word that always makes my insides somersault]
in her only kidney.
Sukoon is now also
running short on time.

But, luckily for Sukoon,
she has me!
I have an extra kidney, I tell the doctor.
Sukoon just needs one healthy kidney . . .
just one, right?
I can give Sukoon my extra kidney!

It isn't that simple,
the doctor interjected.
Along with one healthy kidney,
the transplant also involves
a lot of money . . .
over two million rupees.
Plus, you may not be a match,
despite being her sister.
In which case, we would
also need to find a donor.
But until you have enough
to fund Sukoon's transplant,
we can try medication
and then dialysis
and see how things go.

The doctor scribbled more lab test requests
and asked us to come visit
when we had the reports.

If

Now we have the results
of the lab tests
but no money to go to the doctor.

Khaloo's earnings are
directly proportional
to the hours he spends
picking up and dropping off customers
in his rickshaw.

Last month Arsal demanded a new bicycle
because Tayab, the boy down the street,
got one for his birthday.
Arsal shed a few crocodile tears
and skipped breakfast one Sunday.
Khaloo worked two extra hours
a day
for a week
and brought home
a sparkling new bike
the Sunday after that.

And although Khaloo may not have enough
for Sukoon's treatment now,
IF he wants,
he can work extra hours,
to fund Sukoon's treatment, Khala Ammi says.

Sukoon's Diagnosis

The lab reports could be in another language
and they would make just as much sense.

        Blood Urea Nitrogen = 75

                Intractable Hyperkalemia

Acidosis

           Glomerular Filtration Rate = 10

Renal Dysfunction

                     Nausea

    Therapy-Resistant Fluid Overload

The lab technician's diagnosis
at the bottom

tells us that all the
symptoms can be managed
through medication,
and if that doesn't work,
then through dialysis
at regular intervals.

The things we disclose

when Khaloo is in a good mood:
- Arsal's falling grades
- reminders for the monthly rent
- anything that Khaloo needs to pay for

Handing Over

When I hold Sukoon's reports out
to Khaloo,
which are only a few sheets
of printed paper,

I feel like someone has helped me
with a heavy load of bricks.
I think I see a flicker of a warm smile
when Khaloo sets his teacup aside
and takes the papers from my hand.

What's this? Khaloo demands in his booming voice
even though he's already taken a glimpse.

My body jerks itself backward
as if shielding me from an impending onslaught.

Sukoon's r-r-reports, I stammer.
My words sound frail and feeble
even though I want to sound brave.

Heated Up

Khaloo **SLAMS THE DOOR** after taking one short look at
Sukoon's reports.
He throws out the carom board,
pushes me,
Khala Ammi,
Sukoon,
Irfan,
and even Arsal,
out of his room,
leaving us to melt away
in the heat,
along with our hopes
for Sukoon's treatment.
Even though the electricity
hasn't been turned off,
and it is still bright outside,
it feels like a . . .

BLACKOUT

Worst Day

Despite Pakistan's win
despite our happy dance
despite the yummy korma
despite the rare, rich dessert
despite the game of carom,
today has suddenly turned into
the worst day.
It feels even worse
than the first time Khaloo yelled at me
when I asked him if I could go play outdoors
with Arsal and his friends in the galli.
But it hurts in exactly the same place.
I know Khaloo doesn't like to spend,
but this isn't an expense. . . .
It's a life-and-death situation!
Arsal glares at me,
then at Sukoon,
pelts us with carom discs, and spits his venom,
Thanks a lot for always ruining everything,
before he stomps into our shared bedroom
and slams the door behind him.

Huddle Hug

I scoop Sukoon's and Irfan's
trembling shoulders into one arm
and cup my other arm
around Khala Ammi's heaving rib cage.
I draw everyone in for a huddle hug.
Khala Ammi's eyes tear up.
I'm not sure if they're tears of guilt
(for raising a mini version of Khaloo)
or tears of helplessness.

S e p a r a t e d

Before, we used to be four:
Mama
Baba
Aarzu
Sukoon.
Now we are clumped (into pairs)
MamaBaba, the dead parents

S e p a r a t e d from

AarzuSukoon, the orphans,
who have to live with Mama's sister,
Khala Ammi, her husband, Khaloo,
and her sons, Arsal and Irfan.
Now that it has come to this,
I hope we remain this way:
AarzuSukoon
neverseparated
EVER!
I wish I could do something—
something more than hoping.

Khaloo's Dictionary Definitions

Extras (n.): runs awarded to the batting side due
to illegal deliveries from the bowling side.
Runs that could cost the bowling side a win.
Runs that should be avoided at all cost.

Extras (n.): expenses incurred on nonessentials.
Expenses that cost Khaloo his peace of mind.
Expenses that should be avoided at all cost.

Extras (n.): the way Sukoon and I feel in Khaloo's house.
Extras that cost Khaloo his peace of mind.
Extras that should be avoided at all cost.

Sunday

I'm glad the next day is Sunday,
the day I have the most chores—
no time to think about Sukoon's illness
or how things will work out.
I need to get a lot done:
- A week's worth of ironing
- Arsal's science assignment (which I'm looking forward to doing)
- Sweeping and mopping the entire house once Sukoon has dusted down the furniture (I will probably dust today since Sukoon's legs are too swollen.)

In addition to helping with
breakfast,
lunch,
dinner,
like I do every day.

While Khaloo naps

in the afternoon,
I am sweeping the balcony
when I notice Khala Ammi stuff something
under her kurta, into her bra.
For safekeeping because women's kurtas
have no pockets, Mama used to say.
The bulge on her chest isn't obvious
once she drapes a flowy black chaadar
over her dupatta.
I'm going next door to Bano's house
to borrow some sugar.
Tell Khaloo if he wakes up.
But I'll be back before he does!
Khala Ammi should know
that I know
that there's a kilo of sugar left!
I'm the one who goes to the bazaar with her
for weekly groceries.
I nod anyway.

Arcs of Hope

I return my focus to sweeping the floor.
I trace an arc with each sweep of my jharo,
like a rainbow, the symbol of hope.
I pray, I wish, I dream,
that we find a way to pay for Sukoon's treatment.
When I'm done sweeping,
I fold and unfold
Sukoon's lab report.
I blow a prayer onto it,
almost willing it to share better news
the next time I unfold it.

Monday

My favorite day of the week is Monday.
And my favorite part of every weekday
is a little before the sun is completely up.
I rise with the birds,
while the house is still asleep.

I say my Fajr prayers
in our shared bedroom
in the sliver of space
between Sukoon's and my shared mattress
and Irfan's and Arsal's mattresses
before it is too bright.
I tiptoe into the common area outside the bedrooms
and roll each piece of
the previous day's laundry
into a ball
and bowl it into an empty bucket,
mimicking the bowling action of Hassan,
my favorite Pakistani spin bowler.
Khaloo's and the boys' white cotton shalwar kameezes
and white prayer caps go into a separate bucket
so they don't get stained by the color of our other clothes.
I carry the buckets into the washing area,
a strip of mini balcony
outside the kitchen.
I sprinkle two scoops of washing powder
into each bucket
(I've decided it is just the right amount)
and leave the clothes to soak
for twenty-five minutes

(I've decided it is just the right amount).
I fill the other four buckets we own with water
so we have enough to use for the next twenty-three hours,
when the water valves in our building
will be closed for the day.
I'll carry two of these to the
only bathroom in our apartment when needed.
I hopscotch my way over the buckets
and head to the kitchen to put on
a pot of water to boil for chai.
When the bubbles rise and pop at the surface,
it is time to drop in the tea leaves,
one
        two
                three teaspoons full
(I've decided it is just the right amount).
The tea leaf specks dive and surface instantly,
collecting at the center of the pot
as if vying for a special spot.
They lend their color to the bubbling water
d i f f u s i n g   s l o w l y,   e v e n l y.
The color of the tea deepens as it brews
to the perfect shade of red black.
I pour in two and a half ladles of fresh buffalo milk
that I boiled the previous night

in a steel daighchi
(I've decided it is just the right amount).
I'm careful not to break the thin film of cream
that blankets the surface of the milk.
(That's the bit that goes into a cup for Khaloo's tea.)
The cloudy swirls of milk soon blend in,
giving the perfect shade of karak chai.
I sieve it through a metal mesh into a thermos
and set it at the table with cups,
teaspoons, and a pot of sugar.
I fry two frozen parathas for Arsal in a pan
and three for Khaloo
in sizzling ghee.
While I sip my morning tea,
I nibble at the crispy edges
of the shami kebabs that will
be flattened into the parathas to form kebab rolls.
I top up our water bottles
from the earthen clay dispenser.
I lay out Arsal's ironed uniform
and wake him so he can get ready
for Khaloo to drop him off at school
before Khaloo goes to work,
picking up and dropping off passengers
in his rickshaw.

Before I get ready for school

I rinse out the clothes,
making sure I remove all the excess water
so the bucket of laundry is easy to lug to the rooftop,
where the clothes will dry.
As I hang out the last of the items,
I hear Khaloo hollering
from our apartment, two floors below.

Like a stray cat
moving with silent, calculated precision,
I descend one flight of stairs
crouching, careful not to let my shadow
give away my presence.
I lean forward, listening closely for signs of danger.
I didn't need to lean.
Loud swearing is followed by taunting,
I should never have agreed
to let those rascals into my house.
The THUD of furniture
swung against concrete-plastered brick walls
makes me fall backward.

Arsal's scurried footsteps
followed by Khaloo's stomping ones
and a loud bang of the door
tell me they have left the house.
I wait for them to exit the building
before I tread down gingerly.

I think I hear Khala Ammi sob
behind the closed door of her room
as I hurriedly change into my uniform.
I knock softly at Khala Ammi's door,
but she doesn't open it.
I leave a soundless kiss
on Sukoon's forehead
(thankfully, she slept through the yelling)
and grab a pack of biscuits
and my water bottle
before I leave home
to walk to my school.
To spend six whole hours
with my best friend, Nazia.

Private School

Arsal has gone to private school,
a coed private school,
ever since he started school five years ago.
Khala Ammi put her foot down
and started embroidering clothes
to pitch in for household expenses,
so Arsal could go to a good school
where he'd be treated well,
where they wouldn't beat boys
who weren't *intellectually inclined*
(as my mama would've gently put it).
In Arsal's school
they have games:
cricket, badminton, hockey.
New sports equipment
and field trips, too!

Public school

is the school I attend.
It's an all-girls public school
because public school is free.
But since it's run by the government,
we have ghost-teachers for some subjects.
These teachers have names
and they have subjects they should be teaching,
but we've never seen them
and probably never will!
Nazia, my best friend since I moved to Khala Ammi's,
tells me they do exist!
They come to collect their paychecks
on the third of every month.
Nazia's mom used to be a teacher—
a real one, not a ghost one—
so she knows.
Why would anyone do that? I asked.
Easy money, silly! Nazia said.
Nazia always seems to know
the kind of stuff I don't.
And her favorite thing to do

is to give me her *I-told-you-so* expression
when something she's already told me about
comes true.
Public schools have no excursions,
but at least we have cricket.
And even though
       it's a worn-out bat
And even though
       the wickets are tree branches hammered into a dirt path
And even though
       the protective guards don't protect much
And even though
       our play area isn't a real cricket ground,
at least we have
somewhere to play.

Nazia

The first day I attended school,
nearly a year ago,
Nazia sized me up
after math class.
You, larki, you're book smart!

Book smart is no good, girl!

Not in this place, at least!

Street smart!

I grinned.

I grimaced.

Then what is?

From that day on,
Nazia made it
her personal mission in life
to teach me how to be
street smart.
I hadn't signed up for her lessons,
but I didn't dislike them either.
It was part of being Nazia's friend,
and I was overjoyed to have a friend.

Nazia says

1. *It's easier to ask for forgiveness than permission!*
2. *Everything is relative!*
3. *Work smart, not hard!*

And although
I don't completely understand
what she means,
just like everyone does
what "Simon Says,"
I do
what Nazia says.

Achaar

Mama used to make achaar
before summer set in each year,
when the mangoes were still
green,
tangy,
raw.

It was a daylong tradition.
All the ladies of our neighborhood gathered,
knotted their dupattas at their waists,
unconcerned about covering their hair,
without any males around.

With their hair in tight buns or braids,
the ladies took their positions,
a perfectly synchronized assembly line.
Some washed raw mangoes.
Some peeled the garlic.
Some grated the carrots.
Some slit the chilies.
Some mixed the masalas.

All sprinkled spice onto gossip.
All laughed aloud.

Once everything was
measured,
weighed,
mixed,
it was
poured into jars,
tightly sealed,
left on rooftops for the sun to do its magic.

Making pickles and chutneys
that would last the year
to be relished with daal and shami kebabs

was an excuse.

It was really their day to

talk,

gossip,

laugh,

and make memories that would last the year.

It would be three weeks before

a lid was undone

to check if each of the vegetables

had fermented enough

to lend its flavor to its neighbors,

to blend into the rest

so they all seemed part of the same

unanimous whole.

Mama always said

it's how it works

with people too;

if they stay close

for long enough,

they rub off on each other.

Mama Was Right

It's how it worked for me and Nazia.
In just three weeks
of knowing one another,
our flavors had diffused.
Some Nazia-street-smartness
had rubbed off on me,
and when Nazia's grades began improving,
I was proud that some of me
had rubbed off on her.

The streets

ring with chatter and high fives,
just like they always do
on the first weekday after a victory.
Everyone has a highlight from the game
they want to share with others.
Uncle Sargham,
the roadside shoe polisher,

congratulates everyone passing by.
He offers a free shoe or sandal polish
in celebration of Pakistan's victory.
I nod in his direction
on my way to school,
acknowledging his offer,
and muster half a smile
and a faint, *Salam-alaiykum.*

Zoned Out

Despite today being Monday,
my favorite day of the week,
everything has been a blur.
From waking up several times during the night
to cold sweats and Sukoon's groans
and swollen limbs,
to school;
when Ms. Lubna, our math teacher,
zooms in on me, her star student,
to solve the sum on the blackboard,
I am a million light-years away,

swirling in a galaxy
of slamming doors
and meteor showers of
Khaloo's *girls should* and *girls shouldn't* rules.
The digits on the board
remind me of Sukoon's lab reports.
I'm sucked into a black hole,
spinning in a whirl
of senseless words and numbers.
Manipulating the numbers on the board
to arrive at an answer seems worthless
when I cannot figure out a way to
manipulate the data on Sukoon's reports
to help her return to health.

Downtime

When the bell rings for science class,
for the first time ever,
I am grateful for ghost-teachers.
I take my journal out of my book bag
and flip to the second half.
My words stumble forth
like the ink that flows
from my drying-out fountain pen:
        splotchy
        scratchy
        rough.

Lies

It has   been 12 months,
that is   365 days,
that is   525,600 minutes
since the earth   quake
that lasted   all of
twenty-seven   seconds
took away MamaBaba
FOREVER.

> The saying *Time is the best healer*
> is a lie!
> The worst lie
> I've ever heard
> in my twelve years.
> Time is not healing our hearts
> since losing MamaBaba.
> Time is not healing Sukoon.
> It's only making things worse.

Sukoon's Disease

I don't know what illness Sukoon has
or doesn't have.
All I know is that
Sukoon is
ALL I have.
I'd do anything—
I'd give anything—
to save her.
But
will anything I give
be enough?

Prison

Khaloo's home is like a prison cell.
Having been born in the mountains,
I never liked the city,
but that isn't why it feels
like a prison cell.

Khaloo has rules for us girls
that make no sense.

He won't let Sukoon and me
leave the apartment after dark,
even though other girls
go to get snacks from nearby shops.
He has threatened to skin us alive if we do.

When I give my opinion on anything,
even pitching in
my views on a game of cricket,
I am shushed.

He taunts Khala Ammi
about how she hasn't trained me well,
about how I don't rinse out the detergent
from the clothes properly
and always drop too much tea
when I pour it into the thermos,
and yet he insists that I do all of this anyway.

He keeps special snacks and even honey

locked away in a metal tijori
that only he can unlock
for himself and to give to Arsal and Irfan.
He makes sure they gulp the treat down
in front of him
so they can't share any with us!

When we had recently moved to Karachi,
I pleaded for permission to go watch a match
at the National Stadium.
He refused.
I told him my baba would take us often.
And pointed out that they even have a women's enclosure at
    the stadium.
Khaloo retorted,
Rules might've been different in your father's home,
but things work the way I want them to around here.
He also asked Khala Ammi to teach me manners,
said I shouldn't argue with elders.
I had to stay out of his sight,
locked in the children's room,
for an entire week
so my presence wouldn't remind him of the argument!

Cricket Is Life	Life Is Not Cricket
Cricket is fun.	Life is not fun.
Cricket is energizing.	Life is not energizing.
Cricket is you, Baba.	Life is empty of you, MamaBaba.
Cricket is fair.	Life is not fair.
In cricket you have boundaries.	In life, too, you have boundaries.
The boundaries apply to all.	But the boundaries don't apply to all.

        I wish life was cricket!

Spill

Nazia watches my face
but doesn't interrupt
as I fill page after page of my journal.
When I'm done,
I cross my arms on the desk in front of me
and bury my head in the gap
between my chest and arms.
Nazia places a hand on my shoulder.
A long, firm squeeze
makes me lift my head
to her wide eyes
that ask me to speak.
I think of holding back
like I usually do,
bottling up my feelings inside
and swallowing my hurt
with my anger.
But, like clumsy hands
carrying a sack of heavy,
overripe tomatoes
that weigh my entire frame down,
I spill

every

single

emotion

without saying a word—

I open the second half of my journal.

The hurt I've been bottling up inside

                              tumbles out.

My gut feels **stretched** and squeezed

all at once.

My words lie exposed

       like overripe   tomatoes

  sprawled   on the   sidewalk

that   will be   trampled   any minute

          by a   passerby.

True Friend

But Nazia does not trample over
the emotions
I've spilled onto the pages.
She sits beside me
and waits until my eyes are no longer rivers.
Then she blurts . . .

What Next?

Quick, let's think of options.
We're running out of time.
Urdu class is in ten minutes, says Nazia.

>Sukoon is running out of time
>to live!
>The reality of this hits me
>only after the words leave my mouth.
>I cup my shivering shoulders into a hug.

Yes, but you can't just sit here and cry.
You have to find a way to earn money!

>Khaloo doesn't even let me play outdoors.
>He'd never let me go out to earn!

Your khala ammi earns.
She does embroidery.
Does it pay well?

>I don't know!
>Besides, I'm no good at it,
>and I don't even like doing that stuff!
>I need the kind of work you can only get
>outside—
>work that only boys can do!
>No one takes girls seriously.

I KNOW this for a fact!

Rubbish!
You can't wish for things
and then do nothing to accomplish your goals!
You can earn, indoors or out,
wherever you wish,
however you like!
You are tougher than you think!

You don't know my khaloo. . . .

Practical

If you asked me
to describe Nazia
in one word,
I'd choose:
PRACTICAL.
Because there is no denying:
she IS right!

Options

Nazia takes my journal,
flips to the next page,
and draws up a list:
1. Sell rotis.
2. Work at neighborhood chai café.
3. Tutor neighborhood kids at home.

Impractical

For someone
as practical
as Nazia,
this is the MOST impractical
list on this planet!
But I don't tell Nazia that,
because there's no point
arguing with Nazia.
I stuff my journal back into my bag.
I'm glad it's time for Urdu class.

Impossible

At home, after school, I find a note
scribbled by Khala Ammi
on the back of one of Arsal's worksheets.

Sukoon swelling too much
Gone to doctor
Lunch on stove
Make roti
Arsal with friends
Irfan with me

I take out my journal
with an urge to tear off the page
with Nazia's list,
but that would loosen the binding,
and I don't want to ruin my journal.
I hear Sukoon's soft whimpers in my head,
urging me to reconsider my options,
for her sake.
I go over each point and add my comments:
~~Sell rotis.~~ Making rotis for three is bad enough! Who'd buy

oblong ones anyway?

~~Work at neighborhood chai café.~~ If only I was a boy!

~~Tutor neighborhood kids at home.~~ Our house is too small to have anyone else over.

Possible

I unfold Sukoon's lab report
(which I guess Khala Ammi forgot
to take along when she must've rushed Sukoon
to the doctor)
and run my fingers over the last few lines,
the doctor's comments:
symptoms can be <u>managed</u>.
Maybe through medication?
Maybe through dialysis?
If anything will make it possible for Sukoon to live a healthy life,
I will do all it takes to collect money for it.
I will do all it takes for Sukoon.

Try

I look back at the list.
Let me give this roti-making a serious try.
For Sukoon!
I roll up my sleeves
and try to roll out each dough ball
with Khala Ammi's precision.
It comes to her so effortlessly,
but I struggle.
Roti #1 looks like part of it fell under a rickshaw tire—
> flat and thin on one side,
> bulgy and thick on the other.

Roti #2 looks like the boot-map of Italy.
> How did I even manage that?

Roti #3 tears at the center.
> ARGH!

I am NOT selling rotis!
I blink away my tears of frustration
at my roti-making skills.
I flip my knife in the air
and slice raw onions at lightning speed instead,
pretending I am head chef at the dhaba down the street!

Chuck,
chuck, chuck,
chuck, chuck, chuck!
I wipe the tears
that sting my eyes
and roll down my cheeks.

Sukoon's face

is unrecognizable when she gets home
two hours later from the doctor.
Khala Ammi says,
They've given her steroids.
I forgot the lab reports
and didn't know where you kept them either,
so we'll have to pay the doctor another visit.
I don't dare to ask, only wonder,
where Khala Ammi got the money
for the doctor's fees and medication.

Pale

Pale ...
the color of milk tea
with too much milk
and not enough tea.

Pale ...
the color of the murky film
that forms over a curry
two days too old.

Pale ...
every story
that is not read by you,
Mama.

Pale ...
every day that is lived
in your absence,
MamaBaba.

Pale ...
the color of Sukoon's skin

that was once
rosy and pink.

Pale . . .
a faintness that leaves a color barely fit
to be called a color
at all.

Lunch

Khala Ammi sinks into a chair.
Her forehead is filled
with worry lines,
in addition to sweat beads the size of sesame seeds.
Irfan hurries to fetch cold water
for Sukoon and Khala Ammi.
He sprinkles some onto their faces,
baked in the sun to a tomato red,
before handing them their glasses.
I set out the aloo sabzi
that Khala Ammi cooked
and the rotis that I made,
which are far from round,
far from anything
anyone will ever pay money for.
Khala Ammi doesn't even notice.
Without saying the dua
of thankfulness
like she usually does
before taking her first bite,
she senselessly piles

bite

upon

bite

into her mouth and swallows

them down with a glass of water.

Sting

When the long day
finally winds down
and a cool evening breeze whistles through our lane,
I open the balcony door
to air out the house
from the stench of onions, sweat, and sabzi.
A welcome, salty breeze,
typical of the Karachi seaside,
sweeps through the house
and catches in Khala Ami's dupatta.
Her face finally exposed . . .
her left cheek, the dimpled one,
is the color of overripe kishmish—
the color of bruised black currants.

Spaced Out

Khala Ammi stares into space.
Whirling questions in my head
bump into each other, but now
is not the time to ask them, nor
to request that Khala Ammi
brainstorm options for making money.
Emotions swell in my chest.
> Anger.
> Helplessness.
> Homesickness.
> Desperation.
> Doubt.
> Guilt.
> Fear.

I escape to our bedroom,
where Sukoon lies on our shared mattress.
My body wants to curl into a small ball.
I bury my head in her lap
like I used to bury my head in Mama's lap.
I hold her swollen fingers, kiss them slowly

and swallow the cork-sized lump in my throat.
I force my lips to repeat the prayer,
as best I can,
that Mama taught me to recite
when I felt caged in.
Too dizzy to search for a tasbih,
I keep count on Sukoon's fading finger joints.
Oh, Allah!
Remove me from the darkness of doubt,
and enter me into the light of understanding.
Throw open for us the doors of Your Mercy,
Oh, All-Merciful!
Sleep slurs my speech,
numbs my emotions,
and brings the whirling questions
in my head to a halt.

When I wake up

the next morning,
there is only one emotion:
DETERMINATION.
It surges within me
like waves on the Karachi beach
during high tide.

More than Aarzu

I am Aarzu
and this is my wish:
I want to be more
than the meaning of my name.
I want to make
all my wishes
come true.

I Have to Earn

I have to let go of my fears.
You are right! I tell Nazia
this morning at school.
She holds my arm,
gives it a tight *you'll-get-through-this* squeeze,
before she flashes me her *I-told-you-so* look
and smirks. *I'm always right!*
I laugh because she is!
During our ghost-teacher class,
she asks about Sukoon.
I tell her about the steroids,
      about Khala Ammi spacing out,
      about the doctor's upcoming appointments,
      about my failed attempts at making round rotis.

                I wish making rotis was as easy
                    as slicing onions, I say.
Seriously? You can slice onions?
Like, superfast? Nazia asks.

            I do! Every day, to fry into birista.
            Don't you have that in your house?
Yeah, of course we do! But my mom doesn't make it herself.

She always restocks it from the weekly Mangal Bazaar.
Ready-made!

                                          People actually buy it?

Of course! Why wouldn't they?

                                        So, people actually sell it?

Yes! And so can you!

Nazia's right! (Isn't she always?)
Fried onions form the base of every curry.
Even though I hate the teary eyes,
I am good at slicing onions
superthin, superfast.
Who wouldn't be
if they had the kind of practice I've had?
Four onions
every day
for a year.
Fourteen hundred and sixty sliced onions
is a ton of practice.
Selling birista should be easy....
This sounds like a plan!

Cricket at School

Since Sukoon's diagnosis,
cricket has been the one thing that
allows me to set my worries			aside.

Nazia and I are the only ones from our grade
who play. So we join our seniors—
Mariam, Tahira, Zeenat, and Ismat—
regularly during recess.
The rest of our batch mates
would rather not get a tan.

If we had enough players to form teams,
    we would have eleven on each side.
    The bowling team would have a bowler,
    a wicketkeeper, and nine fielders.
    The batting team would have
    two batswomen on the pitch,
    one on strike and one off-strike,
    with the rest of the players
    awaiting their turn in the stands.

If we had proper teams,
> we could have a proper match,
> with two innings,
> with each innings being twenty or fifty overs long,
> and each over lasting six balls.

If we had a proper cricket field, we would have
> a twenty-two-yard pitch,
> crease lines painted white,
> boundaries, sixty-five to seventy-five yards out
> from the center of the pitch,
> demarcated by ropes.

But none of this stops us from playing.
> We use a stick or a straw to draw lines in the sand
> to demarcate the shortened crease and boundary.
> We use twigs for wickets and pebbles for stumps.
> We share our only helmet and bat.
> We shorten the game to two overs
> so we are done in half an hour.
> We make two teams:
> Two batswomen form the batting side.
> A wicketkeeper, a bowler, and
> two fielders form the bowling side.

Comet

When it's my turn to bowl during a game of cricket, I back up ten steps behind the crease. Align the first and middle fingers of my right hand on either side of the ball's seam. My mind clears. I laser-focus on the wickets, eyes on the middle stump, aiming for a yorker. I spring forward, full speed. Anticipation fuels excitement. The free ends of my dupatta trail behind me like the tail of a comet in the sky. With a hop I swing my right arm and release the ball. The energy from my springing steps transfers to it. Along with my energy, the blur of the ball carries with it my focus, my anticipation, my prayers.

Earn

Earning is not nearly as easy
as I thought.
After two weeks
of selling my birista
at the weekly Mangal Bazaar, Tuesday Market,
I've barely had time to keep track
of expenses and earnings.
I haven't been able to complete
my school assignments
or help Nazia and Arsal with theirs.
When Khala Ammi takes the money
from my birista earnings
for Sukoon's next lab tests and steroid shots,
I have just enough left over
to buy the next six kilos of onions and
a quart of oil,
and to pay the fee to rent
part of a stall,
splitting it with our neighbor,
Bano Aunty's son,
at next week's Tuesday bazaar.

Equals

Coincidently the cost of ingredients
is also the price for used cricket gear
that is sold in the secondhand section
of the Tuesday bazaar,
at a stall not too far from
where my onions are sold.
I think of asking Khala Ammi—
it would be perfect
if I had my own gear
to wear while I play
cricket at school.
But my wish gets buried
under a long lists of prescriptions
when Khala Ammi rushes Sukoon
to the doctor the next day:
Diovan,
Zaroxolyn,
Lipitor.
Too hard to pronounce.
Too many to remember.

Thursday Ritual

Ever since my parents disappeared
under the rubble,
Khala Ammi sits with Sukoon and me
on our shared mattress
on Thursday nights
just before sunset.
She lights agarbatti and
plucks fresh bougainvillea,
and together we say
the prayer for parents
that Khala Ammi taught us
from the Qur'an.

> *My nurturing Lord!*
> *Have Mercy on both of them*
> *like they nurtured me (when I was) small.* [1]

The smoky smell from the incense sticks
teases my nose,
lingers in our clothes,

[1] Qur'an 17:24

long after the sticks have burned through.
Much like MamaBaba's memory
teasing
lingering
long after they are gone.

Ramadan

When Ramadan rolls around,
Sukoon reminds me
she is old enough for her first fast.
I stroke her head,
remembering how, two Ramadans ago,
Sukoon woke up before dawn
and sobbed, wanting to fast *like Aaru Aapi*.
Mama promised Sukoon
she could fast when she turned five.
Now it is Ramadan
and Sukoon is five,
but there's no Mama
and no way Sukoon can fast
with a single failing kidney.

Guilty

When Khaloo goes back to sleep
after a heavy sehri of lassi, chai, kebabs, and parathas,
Khala Ammi helps me chop onions
so we have double the amount
to sell
to meet the increased demand
for Ramadan and Eid al-Fitr.
Even though Khaloo has granted me permission
to sell fried onions at the weekly bazaar,
Khala Ammi says we shouldn't let him feel
like we are spending
a lot of time preparing the stock that will be sold.
The medication has been helping Sukoon,
and seeing her swelling reduced
lifts a weight from my shoulders
that I didn't know I was carrying.

The day after Eid,
I ask Khala Ammi if I can start saving
for some cricket gear.

She doesn't say no,
but the expression on her face
makes guilt peel away,
layer by layer,
my dreams of ever owning
my own cricket gear.

Sukoon writhes in pain
a week after Eid,
from a burning sensation
whenever she uses the toilet.
We soon learn it is an infection.

When her swelling grows
and her fever spikes,
so does my guilt—
at being healthy enough
to even think of playing cricket.
Khala Ammi has been helping me out,
and even Arsal has stopped begging her for money
to spend on evening snacks
for when he plays with the galli boys.
I guess I should be working even harder
and stop dreaming about games.

Ache

Sukoon hugs me extra hard on days
when I flop into bed
beside her and let loose
my hair,
and the onion-sweat-stench trapped in my braid
                                                    tumbles forth.

Her swollen arms wrap around me
in a feeble gesture of gratitude.
But, instead of drowning out
the exhaustion from the day
like your hugs used to, Mama,
Sukoon's hugs only make me ache
and worry for how I will ever earn
enough for her to get
the treatment she needs to heal completely.
I miss you so bad, MamaBaba.

Totals

When I calculate
the amount I've earned
against the amount I've spent on
- onions
- oil
- rent for the Mangal Bazaar stall
- transport
- Sukoon's appointments and medication ,

I have little left.
And yet whenever I lay my head
on my pillow and feel
the slight stiffness from the rupee notes
inside my pillowcase,
my mind immediately strays to
that secondhand cricket gear.
I guess you can't stop Aarzu
from *aarzuing* for cricket!
I make a mental note
to tell Nazia my clever thought!

Fried Onions

The odor lingers

in my clothes

my armpits

my braid

my dupatta

my school books.

Even the fruit-scented markers

that I won in last year's spelling bee competition

now all smell . . .

of fried onions.

But fried onions are the only

item I can sell

at the weekly Mangal Bazaar

that everyone buys in BULK.

Because who wants to

shed tears slicing onions

when you can simply buy them

for a mere two hundred rupees a bag?

My Braid

My braid is so long, it sways like a donkey's tail that wraps around my hips while I chop, chop, chop onions, making me feel hot, hot, hot despite it being December, supposedly the coldest month of the year in Karachi. I want to use the kitchen scissors and cut my hair short, like Arsal's and Irfan's. (There'd be one less thing that traps the stench of fried onions.) You have your mama's hair. The whole neighborhood envied her braids, Khala Ammi says, and refuses to let me touch my hair. But I cover my hair, I protest. Khala Ammi wants to wax my arms and thread my upper lip and learn how to groom myself. *Aarn beti, you will soon bloom into a young lady.* I wish you were around, Mama, to see me bloom, to help me, to understand me, to watch me make my wishes come true.

Savings

Profit = earnings − expenses.

The equation seems simple.

The more onions I fry,
the more effort I put in,
the more profit I should make.

But even though
I have been selling more and more fried onions,
when I total up my earnings and expenses
and solve the equation,
my profit seems to diminish.

My savings keep dwindling,
even though I'm careful to count my money
before I stuff it safely into my pillowcase.
I count it again when
I hand money to Khala Ammi
the days when she takes Sukoon for her appointments.
I'm good at math, but somehow
I'm not good at keeping accounts.

Measuring Up

As Tuesday approaches
week after week,
I drop my week's worth of hard work
into plastic sleeves
sealed at one end.
I carefully estimate the weight
of the first bag,
remove a few flakes of golden onions,
then add back a couple
until it looks just right.
Every subsequent bag is filled
using my hands
as weighing scales,
measuring the freshly filled bags
against the first.
Now I know,
fried onions also smell like . . .
poverty!

Tears and onions,

onions and tears,
they go together like
a girl and her dupatta,
orphans and nostalgia,
daal chawal and achaar,
poverty and the yearning for wealth.
I thought
I'd get used to it—
that my eyes would grow
tired of blinking away
the tears that well up . . .
but no!
Tears and onions,
onions and tears,
always together.
As long as they keep
Sukoon and Aarzu
always together,
I will carry on slicing,
frying, and packing onions.

Choices

Pakistan is playing another cricket tournament.
Khala Ammi and I usually tune in to the radio
and hear the match commentary together in the evenings.
But starting this Monday,
schools are closed for two weeks
for winter vacation and
Bano Aunty next door
has invited Khala Ammi and us girls
to watch the match together
and indulge in chai and gup shup.
Bano Aunty has a TV, and even though it is small,
it is still way better than hearing the match on the radio.
But then I remember, it is Monday—
the day I need to pack everything for the Tuesday bazaar.
And that means I have no choice but to stay home and work.
And that stinks—even more than onions.

Back-to-School Weekday Routine

1. Pray Fajr
2. Pray and blow duas for Sukoon
3. Wash clothes and fill water buckets
4. Make chai
5. Fix breakfast for Arsal, Irfan, and Khaloo
6. Braid my hair
7. Pin dupatta
8. Leave for school
9. Dread ghost-teacher science period (a waste of time)
10. Rush home
11. Bathe (if there's enough water left in the buckets)
12. Oil my hair
13. Pray Zuhr and Asr
14. Catch up on Sukoon and Khala Ammi's day
15. Teach Arsal (or rather, complete Arsal's homework)
16. Help Khala Ammi prepare dinner
17. Pray Maghrib and Isha
18. Chop onions
19. Fry onions
20. Pack onions (on Mondays)
21. Fill out journal
22. Flop onto mattress

Stained Hands

My hands are
rough with knife cuts
from chop
        ping onions
day after day,
week after week.
I do not complain to Khala Ammi,
because I should be grateful
that I've found a way to earn.
But I wish I could find a way
to make money
to save Sukoon
without cho pp ing, frying, packing onions
using knives, as sharp as Khaloo's words,
that make me teary-eyed.
I hold my hands up,
wet with tears and sweat,
palms facing the cloudless Karachi skies,
and call to Allah,
like you taught me to,
MamaBaba.

Gullak

I buy a clay gullak
for twenty rupees
and draw an onion on it
to save the money
I earn from selling onions.
Arsal's snarky comments
mock my efforts.
Who spends money
to save money?
This gets me thinking.
Why is Arsal so concerned
about my money?
Then it suddenly strikes me:
I am *not* a bad accountant.
My savings have indeed been dwindling.
Arsal's probably been stealing them
to get snacks for himself
when he plays in the streets
with his friends, the galli boys.
I smack myself for not having picked up on it earlier.
That's probably why he hasn't been begging Khala Ammi
for money when he goes out to play these days.

Addition

Khala Ammi has equation-like rules for Arsal.

She began using them

when he turned eleven, last year.

They always go something like this:

Eat your banana + finish your homework = get to play.

No complaints from school + pray salah at the masjid = a rupee
   for candy.

She occasionally uses them for Sukoon and Irfan, too.

But never for me!

It seems the rules of addition

apply to everyone . . .

except me.

Because I am Aarzu,

mature, responsible, samajhdar.

Or at least that's what everyone

expects me to be.

Sometimes I wish I could get a break

from all the chores

from all the onion cutting

from all the expectations

from being the eldest.

Sometimes I wish Khala Ammi's rules applied to me too.
Finish washing the clothes + teach Arsal = you can play cricket . . .
outside!

I remind myself

Allah does not place
a burden heavier than one can carry
on anyone's shoulders.

But my shoulders are growing tired
of all the responsibility
that they're carrying.

Division

Addition isn't the only math rule
that doesn't apply to me.
Today, the second day of the New Year,
is Match Day again.

Khala Ammi has made her delicious biryani.
She's carefully counted six botis
so each of us will get one chunk of meat.
I pray it will be a celebratory meal,
but Pakistan loses the match,
and this lands Khaloo in a particularly bad mood.

At dinnertime he yells at Khala Ammi,
Shut off the extra lights around the house.
You all squander my hard-earned money.

Stop helping in the kitchen, he barks at Irfan.
Aarzu is here for that work.
He calls to Arsal,
Shut your room door. I'm tired of hearing that sickly child whimper.

I run back and forth
between the kitchen and the dining table,
fetching cold water, sharbat,
and more kachumbar salad for Khaloo.

While I top his glass with water,
he fishes out a second boti
from the heap of flavorful basmati rice,

looks straight at me,
eyes full of spite,
and drops the boti onto his plate.
You earn now—
you should pitch in
for household expenses.
Until you do,
no botis for you.

Looks like the year is off
to a bad start already.
Looks like division
doesn't apply to me either.

Recurring Dream

Khaloo is the batsman.
    I am the fielder, staked out
        at the field's farthest edge, the boundary.
        Khaloo whacks the ball.
        I leap into the air
                s t r e t c h my arms

                              enough to
                           S-C-R-A-P-E
                        my nails against the ball,
                    keeping it from
                 crossing the boundary,
             keeping Khaloo from
       scoring a sixer.

                    U
            R   P
The crowd E   T S in applause for me.

Straw Strategy

Khala Ammi has invented a new totka
to treat Sukoon's kidney dysfunction....
A straw!
This will help her kidneys function better.
The water will flush away all the nasty stuff,
Khala Ammi claims.
She buys a fancy straw
(that I'm sure she saved up for),
loopy spirals,

sunshine yellow—
Sukoon's favorite color.
Khala Ammi instructs me
to refill her glass
every time it is empty.
I hope her totka works,
but I have a sinking feeling,
this time . . .
it won't.
The more water she drinks,
the more swollen she looks to me.

Peeking In

On the way back from school,
on the first Friday
after two weeks of winter vacation
(which were a blur of onion chopping),
I walk beside Nazia.
My thoughts flit from
Sukoon's upcoming appointment
                                    to onion cho pp ing and frying.

Nazia elbows me.

Dekho, dekho!
Look na! I've heard there's a wedding coming up at this bungalow.
Look how they are stringing up the lights . . . ufff!
Imagine how beautiful they'll look in the night.
Aray, come here.
Nazia pulls me behind a bush
across the road from the bungalow.
We stare, gobsmacked
at the grandeur of the bungalow,
as the gates fly open.
A siren blares,
telling passersby to make way.
Guards hang out of black jeeps
that are part of the VIP patrol
flanking a single sparkling-white Prado.
The image of a pearl safe in its oyster shell
from Arsal's science book
flashes in my mind.
Bulletproof! Nazia whispers,
then sucks her front teeth in disapproval.
And yet so much security!

First Glimpse

The gates to the bungalow
swing shut faster than they opened.
The loud THUD
makes me jump.
Oye larki? Kia karr rahi ho?
An armed guard calls to me,
twirling the edge of his mustache
as I stand beside the bush
opposite the bungalow's entrance,
forgetting to hide myself
and my surprise
at the bungalow's glory.
It's the first time I have witnessed this beauty
hidden behind high boundary walls.
A forbidden world amidst the slums.
A barbed-wire mesh borders the walls,
which Nazia says is rumored to carry
a high-voltage electric current
to fend off potential robbers.
Nothing, nothing, Nazia confesses to the guard.
Yeh nafsiati mareez hai!

Nazia explains that I'm a patient
suffering from some kind of memory loss
and pretends she is my gracious guardian.
I am not! I protest in Urdu
through gritted teeth.
Nazia elbows me to keep silent.
That's what they all say!
Her grin is stitched onto her face
as she locks our arms at the elbows
and pulls me away from the bungalow.
Oye! Bachay, if you know any boys your age,
get them. We need helpers around the house.
Sahib has given instructions
to spread the word for helper boys.
It's a shaadi ka ghar.
Wedding's coming up in a few months.
Sahib pays very well!
calls the gatekeeper after us,
rubbing his thumb and first finger
as if counting the rupee notes that
an employee earns at the bungalow.
My ears perk up.
This could be the perfect opportunity—
I could earn more money.

Nazia drags me toward home
while giving the guard a thumbs-up over her shoulder,
acknowledging his request.

Furious

How dare you? I scream.
I'm furious for being called forgetful
and used as the scapegoat
when it was her fault we stopped
to sneak a peek in the first place.
But most of all, I am upset
at being dragged away.

Nazia claps her hands together,
pleading my forgiveness.
So dramatic!
I saved you, yar! she rationalizes with me.
*They would've skinned us alive
if I hadn't made up an excuse!*

I roll my eyes.
The guard sounded quite friendly,
not threatening at all!

Nazia pinches the skin of her throat,
the way she always does
when she's making a promise.
The family is mighty powerful
and very influential.
Sahib is a politician—
he has connections right to the top!

I scoff at her exaggerations.

On the Way Home

Nazia keeps repeating her apology,
slamming her book bag against mine,
"accidentally" colliding with me,
joining her hands together,
trying to ensure I am no longer upset.

I slap Nazia's pleading hands aside.
Cut the drama, I say, and keep walking.
I kick a pebble ahead of us,
and Nazia kicks it back.
We continue our pebble game
until we reach her lane.

Nazia winks and giggles.
The bungalow was cool, na?!
I nod.
Our eyes are glassy again
from the dazzle of the sparkling vehicles.
Wasn't a glimpse worth being called nafsiati for?

I pick a pebble up from the dirt road
and fling it at Nazia playfully.
Nazia sticks her tongue out at me
and runs into her building, laughing,
while I shuffle in the direction of my home.

Debating

The whole weekend
    while I wash the dishes
    while I iron clothes
    while I comb my hand through Sukoon's hair
    while I trace arcs with my jharo as I sweep the floor
    while I make Arsal complete his school assignments
I imagine what it would be like to work at the bungalow.

If only I was a boy . . .
oh, the money I could earn
for Sukoon's treatment
and maybe even
for my cricket equipment.

If I Was a Boy

MamaBaba,
did you ever pray that I was born a boy?
Did you ever secretly hope for one
when you were going to have Sukoon?
Did you ever wonder about
the world of opportunities
that was shut for us
when we were born girls?
How did you laugh
and dress us up
and braid our hair
and celebrate us every minute,
knowing what hardships we would face?
Or did you dream of fighting the inequalities
we were bound to endure
in this land of ours?
Or were things different where we lived?
Did gender not matter
up in the mountains?
Were girls an asset too?
Why do I feel like such a burden?

Possibility

While I fry batch after batch
of onions on Saturday,
an idea sizzles in my brain.
In that instant, I wish
I could confide in Nazia.
I need a game plan.

I almost blurt out the seeds of my plan to Khala Ammi,
but Nazia's words remind me:
It's easier to ask for forgiveness than permission.
My lips stitch themselves up,
not letting a single word slip.
My lungs pull air, hot, steamy, laden with oil
into deep belly-breaths
that feel oddly light
with the excitement of possibility.

It's the same feeling I get
when I know Pakistan
is about to win a match.
Bubbles of hope rise within me
like the fizz of a just-opened can of Pakola soda.

While I'm doing my homework

on Sunday afternoon,
humming a tune and
gazing out the living room window,
dreaming of the opportunities
that are waiting for me
if I'm able to disguise myself
as a boy,
Irfan hops behind my chair.
Aaru Aapi, I've never seen you so happy!
he says over my right shoulder.
Did you get back your school test results?
he says over my left shoulder.
The test that I made dua for? he asks in hushed tones,
    careful not to disturb Khaloo's Sunday afternoon nap,
    careful not to let Arsal overhear,
    careful not to wake Sukoon.
Yes, yes, that's right! I say.
I am happy! So, so very happy.

I swing around,
lift Irfan,

spin him around and around,
until we both fall over,
giggling!

Corn Silk

When Khala Ammi returns
from chatting with Bano Aunty next door,
she has a childlike skip in her step
and a kilo of corn
with the husks still on.
She plucks and boils
golden strands of corn silk.
This totka is tried and tested!
Khala Ammi assures us.
Bano's sister's daughter-in-law
had a neighbor
whose kidney problems vanished
when he used it!
A now-awake Sukoon scrunches her nose.
I laugh inside, seeing Khala's excitement
and Sukoon's distrust and disgust.

Uniform

On Monday morning
I choose to wear my baggy uniform,
the one that is two sizes too big,
the one without my school logo
on the front.
I pack a paper bag
into my book bag.
I can barely wait to tell Nazia my plan.

Trust

When I leave home,
    I tell Khala Ammi I will be staying after school
        from now on to help Ms. Lubna, my math teacher,
        write out and correct worksheets.
    I tell Khala Ammi not to wait for me for lunch.
    I tell Khala Ammi I will complete my chores when I get home.
She cups my face in her warm hands,
kisses me on my forehead,
kiss upon kiss.

She tells me I am a good girl,
a hardworking girl.
Your parents would've been so proud of you, Aaru.

She says she trusts me,
but I am not ready to trust her. . . .
I fear she might get in trouble
if Khaloo finds out she knew.
I fear she might get in trouble
if Khaloo thinks she was in on my plan.
I fear she might not approve of me
disguising myself as a boy.

Confiding

The first chance I get
to share my plan with Nazia
is during a ghost-teacher class.

Her eyes widen but so does her smile.
Are you crazy? No way!
I half expect her to stop me
before I continue,
but she only cheers me on!
Now, that would be cool!
Until I tell her she needs to help me
chop off my hair.
Because there is no way hair
that wraps around my waist
like a donkey's tail
is getting hidden under a turban.
No way! THAT is crazy!
You can't be serious?
What will your Khala Ammi say?

She won't find out! I say in my *as-practical-as-Nazia* tone.

Nazia clicks her tongue,
taps her temple with her index finger,
as if telling me,
Smart thinking!

A Connection Lost

After telling Nazia,
I take the paper bag from my schoolbag,
borrow a pair of scissors
from the teacher's desk,
and ask Nazia to follow me
to the dingy bathrooms
that have no mirrors.
They are no more than
a couple of holes
in the mud-packed earthen ground
with chipboard dividers that are
stained and scribbled on
with bathroom jokes in Urdu.

I hand Nazia the scissors.
A beam of sunlight
from the straw-thatched roof
deflects off the scissors' blades.
A glint of power flashes in Nazia's eyes.
I s l o w l y remove my dupatta from my head
and hang it on a divider.

I hold my breath,
half hoping Nazia refuses
to chop my braid.
But before I can breathe out . . .
Khuch. Khuch. Khuch. Khuch.
My burgundy locks fall to the ground,
followed by
tupp, tupp, tupp, tupp.
My tears.
I dump the half-tied braid into the paper bag
and dump the paper bag into the trash bin.
I bury the braid my mama used to oil for me
beneath tissues and wrappers.
Sorry, Mama, I whisper.
Before we leave the washroom,
I entomb the remaining hair on my head,
barely touching the nape of my neck,
beneath fold upon fold
of my cotton dupatta.
I tie my dupatta securely
with an extra tuck
under my chin.
I make a mental note
to get more hijab pins.

Secrets

I will not remove my dupatta
even when Khaloo isn't around.
I have never kept a secret from Khala Ammi,
and I never planned to,
but as Nazia says,
Never say never!

Identity Switch

Once our school empties
out for the day
and the school gatekeeper leaves
for his Asr prayers,
I stuff my book bag
into Nazia's book bag.
I tie my dupatta into a turban
and let each of its pallos hang loose
on either side
over my shoulders
down to my chest.
You could just remove your dupatta, Nazia says.
You're a boy now. You don't need to cover your hair!

But I'm NOT a boy.
I AM a girl!
And I need to . . .
I WANT to cover myself
just like my mama used to cover herself.
I want to cover myself
like Islam requires me to.

The Gate

Nazia and I head to the bungalow
and stand at the gate this time.
Golden lion statues guard the entrance.
A bronze emblem flashes
G-8, the house number.
Bright lights automatically switch on
(even though it is as bright as ever outside),
spotlighting anyone who approaches the driveway.
Security cameras click and swivel,
making us their focus.
A robotic voice with a foreign accent says,

> *Step back.*
>> *Step to the right.*

Step to the left—
until we are in full focus
on the security screen.

The main gate swings open
to reveal two more security gates,
which beep and buzz,
daring us to enter.

The same guard as before
appears from behind the gates,
twirling the edge of his mustache.
Salaam, Guard Uncle, Nazia says,
my cousin is available for work.
She adjusts the twice-as-heavy book bag straps
on her shoulders
and straightens her back.
First tell me what you will pay him.
Also, he needs to be home
by six every day, not a minute later.
Nazia speaks loudly, makes herself clear.
Doesn't he speak? the guard inquires.
He does. He's just shy, Nazia says,
placing her hand on my shoulder.
First Chotai Sahib will interview him,
says the guard,
sizing me up
from the top of my turban
to the tips of my fraying sandals,
and Amma will approve.
He makes a thumbs-up gesture.
And only then can I answer all your questions.

I scratch the back of my left leg
with the tip of my right foot,
unsure of what I'm getting myself into.

A voice in my head reassures me,
> *This is for Sukoon.*
> *Soon you'll earn enough,*
> *soon she will get her treatment,*
> *soon she will heal.*
> *You won't have to lie*
> *to Khala Ammi for long.*

Inside

The guard instructs Nazia
with the butt of his rifle—
as if it is the most casual of things to do—
to wait inside the gates.

She lowers herself onto a carved wooden bench,
polished to a deep dewy brown—

the color of certainty,
the same as all the windowpanes on the ivory house.

He marches ahead,
rifle strung over left shoulder. . . .
Follow me, he says.

Right, left, right, left. . . .
I whisper instructions to my feet
that shuffle reluctantly
without Nazia by my side.

We walk the distance from the gate to the front door,
which feels as long as a cricket pitch—
roughly twenty-two yards,
longer than the length of our entire apartment.

The guard stops outside a wooden door
that leads into the house.
Buzz, clink, unlatch.
The door opens magically,
reminding me of stories of the
enchanted caves of Aladdin.

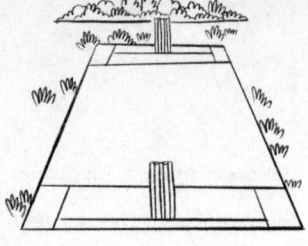

My head bobs
like one of the wooden figurines
on the marble-topped table by the entrance.
I capture snapshots of everything in my mind's eye:
    corridors stretch, linking to longer passageways.
    Long-horned deer heads with marble eyes lurk on every wall
    (so real, the hair on my arms stands on end).
    Vibrant paintings.
    Nude statues
    (that I peek at from the cracks between my fingers).
    More gold lions.
    Dazzling crystal chandeliers
    (the kind I've only seen in the windows of big light shops).
    Fresh fuchsia flowers in sapphire vases.
    Copper-thread-tasseled velvet throw cushions.
    Turquoise curtains draped with scalloped valances.
    High-backed saffron-colored chairs that resemble thrones.

I can't wait to tell Nazia how grand
the house is on the inside.

The guard speaks in a respectful monotone
into an intercom,
Jee, jee acha, jee, Chotai Sahib, jee.

He shows me,
> and my turbaned head,
> and my onion-stench,
> and my faded baggy uniform,
> and my fraying school sandals
> (that I forgot to remove outside the house before I entered),

to a room with ceilings three stories high,
chilled to an uncomfortable temperature,
another reminder of how different everything is
here on the inside compared to everything on the outside
and everything at Khaloo's apartment.

The Interview

I'm not sure which is louder,
the Tish-THUSH, Tish-THUSH
of my worn sandals
(the buckle hanging by a thin sliver of leather and lots of hope)
on the polished marble flooring
or the lup-DUPP, lup-DUPP
of my heart as I approach the boy,

probably a few years older than me.
This is the boy whom the guard
has been calling *Chotai Sahib*, young master.
He holds out his hand to shake mine,
and I'm taken aback. . . .
Girls do not shake boys' hands,
because we are Muslim.
My lup-DUPP-lup-DUPPing heart
beats faster and louder.
I scratch the back of my left leg
with the tip of my right foot,
hold my hand to my chest,
and squat to the ground—
a gesture of humility,
a culturally acceptable way
for a worker boy to show respect to his master.
What is your age? he asks.

Twelve, I say.

Where do you live?

Close by.

How many siblings?

One.

Will you work till six in the evening? he asks.

From tomorrow.

Off on Sundays?

                                        And Saturdays?

A figure behind him
draped in a red-and-blue Ajrak dupatta
places her hand on Chotai Sahib's shoulder
and nods a slow nod
when Chotai Sahib glances her way.
A green signal for me.

                                        Shukriya. Shukriya.

I bow my head and replant
my hand of gratitude on my chest.

Nazia's Questions

Wasn't that a short interview?

                                        Felt too long to me!

Did you get the job?

                                                        Yes.

When do you start?

                                          Tomorrow.

Aren't you happy?

                                            I guess.

My heart would be cartwheeling inside my chest,
but the guilt of all that I'm hiding from Khala Ammi
is barricading the excitement.

What work will you have to do? Fry onions?

I hope not.

Didn't they tell you what you'd be required to do?

Nope.

Didn't you ask?

I forgot.

Are you sure you got the job?

Seemed like they liked the looks of me!

Mode Switch

Nazia walks toward her apartment
and shows me the nook
behind her apartment gate—
where she will leave my book bag after school.
When I am free from work at the bungalow,
I will pick up my bag
and switch back from boy to girl.
I retie my turban into a dupatta.

And transition from
as-free-as-a-boy mode
to culturally acceptable girl mode,
making sure Khaloo, Arsal,
or any neighborhood men
do not spot me.

When I reach home

I draw my dupatta closer and fasten it with a pin,
careful not to prick my skin.
But guilt pierces through me when Khala Ammi asks,
It's so hot. Why don't you loosen your dupatta, Aaru?
I mumble something about an Islamic lesson:
boy cousins aren't exactly brothers,
and that's why I need to cover
myself in front of Arsal.
Khala Ammi beams.
The guilt pUlseS when she says,
I'm so proud of the young lady
you're turning into, Aaru!

I promise

I will tell Khala Ammi
when the time is right.
Oh, Allah, forgive me for lying,
but it's the intention that matters, right?
I'm doing it for Sukoon,
I'm doing it for Khala Ammi,
and maybe for me, too.
I hope she will understand
when I explain my intentions.

Roti Face

When it's time to go to bed,
Sukoon's eyes are little slits
because her cheeks are so **swollen.**
Her face burns with fever
and resembles a fluffed-up roti—
one more reason not to like gol rotis!

No One Asked

As I repeatedly soak and squeeze
a handkerchief in ice water and
dab, dab, dab
it on Sukoon's forehead,
I mull over all the things
Chotai Sahib didn't ask:

- My name
- What work I know
- What work I'd be willing to do
- What I expect to be paid
- Why I need to work.

Chores Assigned

The next day after school,

Amma, the lady in charge of the servants at the bungalow,

takes me from one room to the next,

up diverging staircases,

down converging hallways.

My heart skips beats

as my feet scurry to keep pace

through the maze.

Amma tells me where to dust and clean,

to help myself to tea,

biscuits, and cold water

in the servants' kitchen.

She tells me to be sure to rest

on the charpoys

in the servants' quarters,

which are sprawling rooms

toward the back of the bungalow.

Each room is bigger than our entire apartment,

and even the spare servants' rooms

have attached bathrooms

with running water

throughout the day.

Servants of Servants

If someone had told me
servants could have servants,
I would've laughed out loud
in disbelief.
But it turns out
I am the servant to Amma,
who is a servant herself!

Sukoon's appointments

are growing more frequent
and require more money.
Sukoon is always drowsy,
and her legs ache so much that
she barely leaves our mattress.
I can't remember when she last spoke
more than a few words,
requesting a drink of water,
or asking to be helped to the bathroom,
before she nodded off to sleep, midsentence,
her head hanging to the side.

Chotai Sahib's Little Sister

The next day after school,
I see Zoya, Chotai Sahib's little sister,
for the first time.
Zoya is twelve (same as me).
I know because

her room has a fluorescent yellow license plate
with EST. 2013 embossed onto it in black . . .
same birth year as mine.
I wish I had one of those,
with MY name
and birth year.
I'd also need a room
of my own
to hang it outside.
Zoya doesn't flinch
when I enter her room
with my signature eau de birista trail
that enshrouds
the faint fruity, freshly washed fragrance
of her silky shoulder-tossed tresses.

Own Room

How would it feel to have a room of my own?
How would it feel to shut the world out?
How would it feel to have some space?
How would it feel to decorate the walls as I wish?
How would it feel to have a place to hang my memories and dreams?

My Own Room

Its walls would be decorated with:
 1. News clippings of Baba's name in the sports pages
 2. A photograph of Mama holding me for the first time
 3. Mama's teacher-training certifications (she was most proud of those)
 4. Baba's first Man of the Match trophy
 5. Uncle Baseer Khan's autographed napkin (though I'd need to frame that first)
 6. My last report card (A+)
 7. Our handmade Pakistan flag
 8. Hand-drawn green cricket jersey with my name glistening in gold

I leave space at the bottom
and another page—
space for sunshine
in case I want to hang
more hopes and dreams
in my imaginary room.

Things I notice

when I make the transformation from Aarzu to Azlan (I quite like the name I've given myself):
- The curves on my body are the same as they were three years ago. (Nonexistent.)
- I have too much hair, on my upper lip, my arms, my legs, my knuckles?! (Just like a boy's.)
- Everyone is expecting me to grow into a "young lady"! (The only thing I'm growing is tall.)

Unacceptable

I try not to make eye contact
with Zoya or Chotai Sahib
because at Khaloo's house I've been told,
> unless necessary,
> it's unacceptable....
> *Rich do not mingle with the poor.*
> *Poor do not mingle with the rich.*

Because at Khaloo's house I've been told,
> unless necessary,
> it's unacceptable....
> *Boys do not talk to girls.*
> *Girls do not talk to boys.*

Because I am a boy on the outside
and a girl on the inside
and poor inside out,
I guess it will be unacceptable
for me to talk
to either of them.

Acceptable

But on the inside of the golden lion-guarded gate,
things are completely different from at Khaloo's home.
No one seems to have a problem with me being poor
or with boys talking to girls
or girls talking to boys.
I expected Zoya to be reserved and bratty,
but her words swell with concern.
She asks me my name.
Azlan, I lie,
without lifting my head
(to avoid eye contact).
Nice name.
Have you eaten?
You look starved!

She disappears
and reappears
with a plate of hot samosas,
takes one herself,
and asks me to eat too.

I adjust my turban;

my eyes meet hers.
Gratitude meets empathy.

I can't help but notice
how much Zoya resembles her mom—
from her almond-shaped eyes
down to her sharp nose—
in the photos that crowd the shelves
etched between dresser mirrors,
under glass tabletops,
on photo walls
that I dusted around the house.

Prayer Mat?

When I want to say my prayers,
instead of going to the servants' quarters
all the way in the back of the house,
I ask Zoya for a prayer mat.
Her blank expression makes me wonder
if I asked for too much.
She hunts frantically near a magazine rack.
Her embarrassed expression tells me she doesn't pray.

When Amma provides me with one,
I ask if I can pray at the end of the corridor
away from the bobbing heads of wooden figurines,
away from the lurking long-horned deer with marble eyes,
away from the nude statues and paintings.

Even though there is no one around me
when I start praying,
halfway through my prayers I feel a presence.
When I finish and peek from the side of my eye,
I see flicks of Zoya's hair.
It makes me wonder if she's ever seen anyone pray before.
It makes me wonder if she wants to learn.

Zoya hums a song,

"Free As a Bird."
I think she says it all wrong. . . .
"Free As a Boy"
is the version
I hum all day long.

Zoya's brother

is Faizan,
aka Chotai Sahib,
aka Young Master,
whom I decide
on closer inspection
looks like a comic book character
that's burst to life.
His trapezoid-shaped eyes
have laughter lurking in their corners.

After the interview
I made a mental note
to avoid being alone
in the same room as him.
I can't quite pinpoint why
his looks make me uncomfortable.
Even the mere thought of him
makes the tip of my right foot
scratch the back of my left leg,
scratch,
scratch,

scratch,

no matter how hard I try to stop myself.

Zoya's baba

is *Daddy* for Zoya and Faizan.
They say it like
Da'eee.
I guess it is what they call
their babas in foreign lands,
where, Amma tells me,
they go on vacation
every year.
Sometimes multiple times a year.
Zoya's baba is
BARAI SAHIB,
BIG MASTER,
for the servants
and me.
Though, from what I see in the pictures
and from what I hear from the servants,
he isn't big in build at all.

Zoya's mommy

has taken Zoya's elder sister
to London
to shop for her wedding.
So boring! Zoya says.

So fun! I think.
Don't you miss her? I ask.

Who, Mommy?
She's barely here
even when she is. . . .
Birthdays with friends,
baby showers with acquaintances,
kitty parties with strangers,
yoga retreats and spa dates,
fashion shows and brand launches.
Mommy attends them all.
No time to attend to us!

When will she return?
They were supposed to be away for a month and a half.
It's only been two weeks since they left.
Don't worry, Mommy's return won't change anything for you.
Amma still manages everything anyway.

Eased

Zoya continues,
*Amma is our real anchor;
she makes sure we eat,
puts honey milk and almonds by our bed
when we have our exams . . .
says it sharpens the mind.
Makes sure Da'eee takes his meds.
She can find my undergarments,
socks, and writing materials
with her eyes shut.
She's been with us
since Faizan Bhai was in diapers.
She knows when I'm down
or Da'eee is upset.
Fixes our favorite meals
to cheer us up.
Talks to us
of her childhood,
partition stories and folktales,
sagas of her kids and granddaughters.
It's when SHE goes on leave
to visit her family*

in her village in Punjab
that Faizan Bhai, Da'eee, and I
are truly lost.
We call her back,
often a week or two in advance,
of her scheduled return.
And when she arrives,
we are all at ease.

Dis-eased

The warmth in Zoya's eyes
as she speaks of Amma
and Amma's gentle, firm hand
tilting Zoya's head backward,
lathering her hair with coconut oil,
combing out her tangles,
reminds me of Mama.
My hands grope for my braid
midway down my back,
until I check myself.
I blink back stinging tears. . . .
No Mama and no braid.

The Prophet's words
from Friday Islamic Studies lessons
ring in my ears:
Jealousy is the worst disease.

                                              I am dis-eased!

The Way You Look at Your Hands

A few days after I begin working at the bungalow,
after I'm done with my chores for the day,
Zoya and Chotai Sahib
(who insists I call him *Faizan Bhai*)
sit on either side of me.
I feel secure
as if flanked by friends
rather than Barai Sahib's children.
Zoya says, *Look at your fingernails.*
I stretch my hands out in front of me,
palms facing forward,
fingers wide apart
like crow's feet,

expecting to find them dirty.

Thankfully, my fingernails are clean.

I told you so. I told you so, screams Zoya to Faizan.

Faizan throws his head back and laughs.

Zoya sticks out her tongue,

puts her hands behind her ears,

and wiggles her fingers.

Now pay up! she demands of Faizan.

They give each other high fives

behind my back,

an inside joke

that makes me feel small,

while also reminding me of Sukoon's well-days

and our own inside jokes.

You're a girl!

Boys don't examine their fingernails like you.

They curl their fingertips in!

You're a girl, aren't you? Zoya demands the truth.

Yes, I say, hanging my head in shame for lying.

Don't tell anyone, I plead.

I need the job.

I'm earning for my sister's surgery, I whisper. . . .

Please,

please,

please.

List of Things That Do Not Change

Even though Zoya and Faizan
know I am a girl,
they do not tell anyone . . .
not even Amma.
I wear my turban,
just like I used to.
They call me Azlan,
just like they used to.

Changes at Home

It turns out Khala Ammi's straw strategy
is indeed a failed totka.
The doctor has put Sukoon on antibiotics
and given Khala Ammi a list of things to do:
- reduce salt intake
- increase lentil intake
- increase fruit intake (except for potassium-rich fruits like bananas)

Khala Ammi takes whatever money I give her

when I break the clay gullak
that holds my fried onion earnings.
I used to have to break it
once every two weeks,
and replace it with a new, empty one.
But now that Sukoon's appointments are
more frequent
(sometimes as often as three times a month),
my gullak feels like a used lemon wedge,
yielding less and less
with every squeeze.

Miss

I miss the times
before I started school in Karachi,
when Khala Ammi used to
play cricket with us girls
across the kitchen and dining room
to cheer us up
after Khaloo left for work every day.
I'll be a cricket player like Baba someday,

I'd tell Khala Ammi.
Maybe you will,
Khala Ammi would say
in her hopeful voice, warm like Mama's.

We stopped playing
when I started school
four months after we moved,
around the time when
Sukoon's energy levels
<pre>
         p   d
         l   e
            u   r
               n   a
                 g   o
                   e   s
                     d
</pre>
and her swelling

Don't Miss

But I also don't miss those days,
because that's when we had just moved to Karachi

to live at Khala Ammi's,
and it didn't take long to realize
we weren't on vacation
with my cousins
at our aunt's!
The earthquake
had shaken our world
and replaced our slow mountain mornings
with fast city mornings.
Replaced our evening turn-taking poetry-reading time
with loud Khaloo-screaming huffing-puffing time.
Our Baba-cuddle-and-giggle nightly tuck-in routine
with Aarzu and Sukoon huddled on
a shared mattress,
with no-one-to-
tuck-us-in-at-bedtime
nights.

It's strange that a memory
can make you long for something
and shudder at the thought of it
all at the same time.

The way it's said

makes all the difference.

At Khaloo's home I'm expected to do everything . . .
as if I need to earn my place in the household.
Khaloo ordered Khala Ammi to fire the part-time house help
(who would dust, clean, and do the laundry)
when we moved in.
And all the work that she'd helped Khala Ammi with
was transferred to me.
Even though I want to help Khala Ammi,
I feel resentment surge within me.

At Barai Sahib's I am the house help.
I'm assigned chores,
but instead of being ordered around,
I get to choose which ones I do when.
On days when I can't complete them all in time,
Amma pats my back and says I can catch up the next day.
Zoya and Faizan Bhai plead with her
to let me off early so we can chat.
Even though I'm paid to work, it doesn't feel like a chore here.
Acceptance envelops me.

#TheHashtagLife

Zoya's phone is part of her
like the stench of fried onions
is now a part of me.
If I close my eyes
and try to imagine Zoya,
her high cheekbones
and long lashes
are lit up
by the glow of her screen.
Her thumbs
f l i c k and s
            c
            r
            o
            l
            l,
s
c
r
o
l
l and   f   l   i   c   k

through
her favorite app.
She spends hours
agonizing over just the right hashtag.
#Zoyaneedscoolhashtags
#opentohashtagsuggestions
#hashtagsofinstagram
#hashtaglife
#hashtagthis
#hashtagthat

Cricket Tryouts

Nazia and I read the bulletin board together
on the last day of January.

PAKISTAN UNDER-15 GIRLS CRICKET TEAM TRYOUTS

DATE: 26th March
VENUE: School field
AGES: 11 to 15 years

*Note: All selections will be merit-based.

Squeal!
Hold hands,
stretch arms into a figure-eight,
jump around
kicking up dust
while tracing circles in the school field.
There's finally going to be
nationwide selections
of girls, fifteen years and younger,
to form an Under-15 Pakistani girls team.

And I know from the way Baba spoke about them
that selections are a highly competitive
talent-hunt program.
Selections are conducted in all districts
across the nation,
in different schools,
cricket clubs,
and coaching academies.
I don't know how I'll find the time
to practice more,
to ensure I get selected.
I don't know how
I'm going to convince Khala Ammi,

who will need permission from Khaloo,
to let me play for the Under-15 team
if I get selected.
But nothing's going to stop me
from trying out anyway!

Cricket Fever

Once school reopens
after a three-day break for Eid al-Adha,
it feels like everyone has cricket fever.
No one knows who will be granted permission to play
if they get selected,
but everyone, even girls who never showed any interest in
 playing,
seek out free time to play more cricket in the school field,
and seek out answers to the questions:
> Am I a bowler?
> Am I a batswoman?
> Am I a wicketkeeper?

We have only one helmet
and one set of tattered protective gear,

abdominal and leg pads,
that we take turns wearing.
We don't mind sharing.
At least we get to form proper teams
now that we have more players!

All-Rounder

When it's my turn to bowl,
I experiment;
I switch out my fast bowling action
with a spin delivery.
I take a few short steps and pitch the ball,
imitating the posture and poise
of my favorite spin bowler, Hassan.
The ball bounces, spins, and slices the air,
smashing the three twigs that serve as wickets,
sending the pebble-stumps flying.

When it's my turn to bat,
    I shuffle my feet,
    adjust the leg pads,
    stride forward,

    shift my weight to my back foot,
free my arms—
    WHACK!
    I watch as the ball sails to the boundary line.

When it's my turn to field,
    I cheer on my teammates,
    call out an attacking field arrangement,
    tell Nazia—who is bowling—to pitch short
    so the girl who is batting is baffled
    and forced to take a shot
    that is high, but not calculated.
The strategy works—the ball lands
in my waiting hands.

My teammates cheer:
Aarzu is an all-rounder!

Weekday Routine

1. Pray Fajr
2. Pray and blow duas for Sukoon
3. Wash clothes and fill water buckets

4. Make chai
5. Fix breakfast for Arsal, Irfan, and Khaloo
6. ~~Braid my hair~~
7. ~~Pin~~ Repin dupatta
8. Leave for school
9. Fill Nazia in on previous day's gossip from the bungalow
10. ~~Dread~~ Wait for ghost-teacher science period to play cricket ~~(a waste of time)~~
11. Change dupatta into turban
12. Stuff book bag into Nazia's book bag
13. Maintain safe distance from Nazia (so no one suspects she's hanging out with a boy)
14. Rush to bungalow
15. Pray Zuhr and Asr
16. Complete chores assigned by Amma
17. Leave bungalow at six
18. Rush home
19. Bathe (if there's enough water left in the buckets)
20. Oil my hair
21. ~~Catch up on Sukoon and Khala Ammi's day~~
22. ~~Teach Arsal (or rather, complete Arsal's homework)~~
23. ~~Help Khala Ammi prepare dinner~~
24. Pray Maghrib and Isha
25. Chop onions
26. Fry onions

27. Pack onions (on Mondays)
28. Fill out journal
29. Flop onto mattress

It Feels Like a Dream

Stands of cheering spectators
under cloudless, clear skies.
I march out to the crease.
I take my place on the crease.
I adjust my helmet on the crease.
I scrunch up my jersey sleeves
right up to my elbow crease,
s t r e t c h and f   x and s t r e t c h.
                  l   e
           e   l
               x......................f

The bowler flicks her ponytail,
begins her twenty-yard run
toward the crease.
I am ready.
More than ready.

The red cork ball darts
toward me at three hundred sixty miles per hour, or more.
I stride forward.
Bat touches ball. . . .
It's a . . . six!

Aaru Aapi, Wake Up!

Wake up! It's six! A sleepy Irfan nudges me awake.
The chirping birds tell me I have missed my Fajr prayers.
I drag my feet to the kitchen.
I take my place by the stove.
I adjust my dupatta.
I scrunch up my kurta sleeves
right up to my elbow crease,
s t r e t c h and f x and s t r e t c h.
 l e
 e l
 x......................f

Aye haye!
It was a dream.

Cold

Over the next few weeks
Nazia grows cold and distant
even when I sit right beside her
or drag her out to the field to play.

The cricket trials will be here before we know it!

I want to talk to her
> about cricket
> and if we can somehow practice more during school
> to increase our chances for selection.

I want to tell her
> how hard I am working.

I want to tell her
> Sukoon will be able to get the treatment she needs.

I want to tell her
> how I feel guilty for enjoying work.

I tell her about Faizan Bhai and Zoya every day,
hoping the stories will distract her
from whatever it is that is troubling her.

She listens, but
barely replies.

Faizan's Drone

At the bungalow one evening,
after he flew his drone all afternoon,
I ask Faizan Bhai:
      its maximum range,
      its minimum price,
      its warranty period,
      where it is available,
and tuck away
all the information
for a day when I can get
a drone of my own.
I imagine myself at the center of a crease
on a cricket field
practicing my shots
with a programmed drone
                swooshing overhead,
sneaking to my side,   zooming in,
        recording every action

for me to replay later

and observe my moves

to learn which ones I need to work on,

to learn which shots I need to improve.

Faizan Bhai chuckles at my questions.

He tosses me the controller,

instructs me on how to fly.

I flick the controls

                              up,

            left,   right,

                     down.

Complete control.

My spirits soar

and so does the drone.

The tip of my right foot

no longer scratches

the back of my left leg

when I'm around him.

He takes aerial images

of the mosque next door.

I hover it closer to my apartment building

and get a few clicks

of the clothes drying on our rooftop.

I show Zoya and Faizan Bhai

where I live.

Drones

Drones baffle me.
They soar so high.
If only I could use one
to send letters
to the heavens
to you, MamaBaba.

Close Call

One evening
after I pick my book bag from the nook
behind Nazia's apartment gate
and make the switch
from Azlan to Aarzu
at the corner of Nazia's lane
under a dim streetlight,
I spot someone moving
behind a bush across the street.
I hold my breath
and freeze.
      How will I explain my turban-dupatta?
      How will I convince whoever has seen me
not to tell on me?
A gust of wind blows and carries away
what I thought was a head behind the bush.
It turns out to be a puffed-up plastic bag.

I exhale.
Phew!

That felt like a poorly timed April Fools' joke.

I catch the pullos of my dupatta
and hold them close to my pounding heart.
I wonder how much longer
I can pull this off.

I'm a girl,
and I can do everything a boy can.
Yet I continue to disguise myself
as a boy
to appear able . . .
                    to others.

Someday I will prove
to Khaloo and Arsal
and all our neighbors
that girls are as able as boys,
if not more, I daresay.

Inside Story

Every morning I wait for Nazia to ask me
details about Zoya and Faizan Bhai
and what happens on the other side of the guarded walls.

When she doesn't ask, I tell her anyway.

About Zoya and her millions of shades of nail polish.

> About the lavish meals the inmates of the bungalow eat.
>
> About the framed-photo walls.
>
> About the shopping trips to London.
>
> About the fruity scents of Zoya's mists.
>
> About the hi-fi intercom system.
>
> About the marble flooring.
>
> About the uninterrupted running water.
>
> About the indoor fountains.
>
> About the shaped shrubs in the garden.
>
> About the drone. . . .

No matter how much I tell her,

I still feel as if I'm forgetting some fascinating detail.

And when the brass bell rings for class,

I tell Nazia, *I'll tell you more tomorrow.*

I'm so grateful for a friend like you,

who helped me get a job like this.

But just like she doesn't ask for help with studies anymore,

Nazia doesn't ask for stories either. . . .

Maybe she knows I will tell her anyway.

Sukoon's doctor says

the medication is not enough.
Sukoon needs to start with dialysis now
and may need transplant surgery
sooner than we think
if the dialysis doesn't work.
There are a lot of *if*s and *but*s,
as Khala Ammi puts it,
but I know for sure that
all this means
I need to
work
work
work
so Sukoon has a chance to
heal
heal
heal
so she continues to
live
live
live

and we continue being
AarzuSukoon
togetherforever.

Dialysis

The doctor says
Sukoon will have to start dialysis this week.
Starting at one session per week,
Sukoon will be monitored
and treatments could be more frequent if needed.
He explained to Khala Ammi,
who explained to me,
dialysis will do the work
that Sukoon's kidneys don't.
It will filter from her blood
the excess salt and water
that's causing the swelling.
It will filter from her blood
the excess waste
that's making her sick.
The machine will
clean away all the bad stuff

and leave behind all the good stuff.

That sounds like a smart machine.
I wonder if they have a dialysis machine to filter
out meanness from people—
I'd pay for Khaloo and Arsal
to be hooked up to it!

Free Care

One Saturday Khala Ammi takes Sukoon to SIUT,
Sindh Institute of Urology and Transplantation.
They wait, wait, wait for a token,
then wait, wait, wait for their turn
on the footpath outside the hospital
in hopes of free treatment.
But return after Asr
without seeing the doctor.
Sukoon couldn't manage the heat
or the crowds,
and Khala Ammi was worried
Khaloo would be upset
if dinner wasn't on the table on time.

And rightly so.
Khaloo huffs and puffs
and practically blows the house down.
No need to run after free treatment
if it means neglecting me and my house!

First Dialysis

When Sukoon returns
from her first dialysis
at a private clinic
near our apartment,
she says, *It wasn't SO bad!*
The room smelled like Lysol floors.
The needle pricks felt like mosquito bites.
And my blood went on a roller-coaster ride
in tubes looping this way and that.
They even had a BIG TV, Aaru Aapi—
she flings her arms wide—
that aired Tinku and Minku.
Remember my favorite cartoon, Aaru Aapi?
And the nurse said my insides got a good cleaning

like a bath after a sweaty day.

Khala Ammi wasn't as entertained as Sukoon
when I asked her how it went.
She laugh-snorted,
It felt like watching paint dry.
Maybe that's a good thing. . . .
I haven't sat so idle in a long time,
maybe before Arsal and Irfan were born,
or maybe before I got married.

With my first salary

in my hands,
my mind strays
to all the wonderful things I could do
with all this money.
In my fist I hold
a thick wad of
possibility.
Cricket gear for me.
A new purse for Khala Ammi.

A toy truck for Irfan.

A fruity mist for Nazia.

New nail polish shades for Zoya.

Dolls for Amma's granddaughters.

But all of that

is grossly outweighed by

     A healthy future for Sukoon.

Another Gullak

I buy another gullak

for my bungalow salary.

I draw a bat on this one.

I bury it under my undergarments

in the milk crate that holds my clothes,

deep inside the folds of the largest dupatta I own.

I will keep my secret from Khala Ammi

and keep the bat gullak hidden there until the day

when I have collected enough to fund Sukoon's surgery.

Cricket Journal Update

Between all my chores at home
    and all the time I spend at Zoya's
    and all the weekend bazaar trips to get supplies
    and all the onion chopping, frying, packing, selling,
I am always running
from bazaar to home
    from home to school
        from school to Zoya's
            from Zoya's to home
                from home to the bazaar.
The only time I
    s l o w down
is when I record
the scoreboard,
sometimes while crouching on the balcony,
sometimes on our mattress beside a snoring Sukoon,
in the cricket section of my journal
on days when Pakistan plays a match.

As the pages of my journal fill up,
tournament after tournament,

match after match,
my dream of playing on a proper team
plays on a loop in my brain.
My fingers tingle.
My feet stretch and flex,
preparing for the day
when I can play professionally.
Every time I see
a bowler on television at Zoya's,
my brain takes a snapshot
of the field arrangement
and calculates where
    the bowler should pitch
and calculates where
    the batsman should whack
and reminds me of the strategy tricks
Baba and I would discuss
while watching foreign teams
play each other.
And no matter how busy
I get with earning money,
my passion for cricket
blazes as bright as a fire
with emerald-green flames.

Play?

One night after I finish my chores,
I tiptoe into our bedroom,
trying to be careful not to wake the boys and Sukoon.
I use a small flashlight
to fish my journal out of my book bag.

<< *BOO!* >>

I drop my journal with a start.
Irfan and Sukoon throw off
frayed cotton sheets from their heads.
They giggle and high-five,
celebrating a successful scare.
Aaru Aapi, please play with us.
Irfan draws the ludo board out from under his pillow.
You two haven't yet slept? I scold.
We'll just play with two gotis each instead of four.
Sukoon retrieves the gotis and die from under our mattress.
Please? Sukoon pleads. *It'll be a short game.*
It's been so long since you played with us!
Guilt makes me concede.

Groggy eyes the next morning
don't make me regret the decision.

I didn't realize how much
Irfan and Sukoon had been missing me,
nor me them,
until this simple game of ludo
that Irfan and I let Sukoon win.

F

When we get back our math test,
Nazia has a big red F
the size of the page.

But it is me who crumples my A+ sheet
and hides it away
so Nazia doesn't feel even worse about her grade.

After class I ask her if everything is okay.
She grunts, and I think it's because she is upset

with the F.

But when it's time to go home,
she leaves school
without telling me.

She leaves without taking my book bag,
and doesn't care to walk me
to the bungalow.

I know instantly:
I'm not the only one
who is dis-eased.

Tell Me

After school I wrap my bag into a gathri
and leave it with Guard Uncle at the bungalow gate.
Inside, while I dust Zoya's room,
she kneels on her shaggy purple rug
(that perfectly matches her curtains and bedspread).

She leans forward to her dresser,
stretches one arm out
to her color-sorted nail polish collection,
picks out an emerald-green shade,
sits back down,
tucks her left foot behind her,
rests her chin
on her propped-up right knee, and says,
Now, tell me all about YOU.
She starts with her tiny-toe nail,
smears green onto the light skin
on either side of her nail.
Using the tip of her thumb,
she wipes the smudges clean
in one swift swipe.

I'd normally have hesitated,
but I've been longing to talk to someone, anyone,
since Nazia has grown so distant.
I begin telling her in hushed tones
    of the earthquake,
    of my "Teacher-Aunty" mama,
    of my rising-to-fame cricketer baba,
    of my ailing sister,
    of my shattered home,
and dreams.

In the time it takes Zoya
to paint her ten toenails,
I spill the story of the eleven years
of my existence
before I reached Khaloo's house.

Embrace

Zoya screws her nail polish shut,
rises to her feet, and embraces me
for a long, looooong time.
I blink away tears.
I'm not sure
if they are tears of longing and grief
or tears of joy for facing change.
Zoya's embrace
makes me embrace the new me.
The in-control Aarzu
who will find the strength
to power on!

I CAN do this.
I WILL do this.

Wedding Preparations

When Zoya's mom and sister return from London,
everything at the bungalow
is swept into the tidal wave
that is wedding preparation.
I learn that the wedding is
the week before the cricket tryouts.
Balmy afternoons
turn to a frenzy of florists
and whimsical wedding planners.
Friends, houseguests, and acquaintances
make their appearance,
unannounced.
There is tea to be served,
dirty dishes to be cleaned,
linen to be laid.
I am exhausted.
The only upside of more people in the house is:
enough people to form teams
to play cricket in the evenings.
And even though I do not play,
even though it is just Zoya and Faizan Bhai

and their friends playing each other,
the air feels charged
and makes me wish I could stay on
to watch their game
that stretches well beyond six in the evening.
But then I think of Sukoon
waiting for me,
and Khala Ammi,
who still thinks I'm helping my teacher
every day after school,
and Khaloo and all his rage
if he sees me outdoors after dark.
I rush home like Cinderella
when the bell tolls six p.m.

Things Zoya's Family Keeps Count Of

- The slabs of gold the bride takes with her to her husband's home
- The furniture sets, jewelry sets, gift money, and appliances—dowry from the bride's close family to the bride, groom, and his family
- The calories they consume at each meal
- The likes on their social media status updates
- The sets of bridal lingerie, gowns, shalwar kameezes packed for the bride to take to her new home
- Their trips abroad that year

Things My Family Keeps Count Of

- The kilos of aata we can afford for the week
- The number of passengers Khaloo will transport in his rickshaw each day
- The hours of embroidery Khala Ammi will need to put in each month to make ends meet
- The hours of electricity load-shedding (which always outnumber the hours of electricity provided)
- The number of botis in the korma
- The kilos of onions I will need to fry and sell for Sukoon's weekly treatment

New Chores

As the wedding draws closer,
Faizan Bhai calls his friends more often,
and Zoya invites hers, too.
They play cricket in their s p r a w l i n g garden
that is the size of a cricket field, just for fun.
I wish I could play too,
and squeeze in some more practice
before the Under-15 girls' team tryouts at school.
But Amma assigns me the task
of making snacks
and rushing to and fro,
from garden to kitchen,
from kitchen to garden,
setting up a spread
of pakoras and samosas,
chutneys and ketchups,
chai, freshly squeezed orange juice, and Pakola sodas,
crispy jalebis with dripping sugar syrup
for Faizan's and Zoya's friends to enjoy
between innings.

What a Catch

I bring out a tray of tea cake and jam.
I'm laying it on the table with my back to the field
when screams echo:
Azlan, Azlan, AZLAAAAAAN,
turn around!
Watch out! Ball!
I turn on my heel.
A red cork ball is
heading right at me.
Eyes on the ball,
hands outstretched,
I leap forward,
full length,
and clench the comet-like blur of red
inches above the ground.
With the ball safe in my hands,
my whole body
falls flat onto the field.
I caught it!
For once I am grateful
for my long arms and long legs.
A surge of accomplishment

throbs in my veins,

numbing the pain from impact.

Faizan's friends, who were fielding,

rush over and hoist me onto their shoulders!

Wah, wah, Azlan, zabardast!

What a catch!

They praise my fielding skills.

I shrug off the applause with a casual

I play at school sometimes,

holding on tight to my turban.

Champion for the Day

They take me

lap after lap

around the field

hoisted on a shoulder-throne.

My turban is my taj.

Its free ends

fly behind me like a superhero cape.

I feel free.

I feel fantastic.

I feel I want to feel this more.

On my way home
the surge from my fielding win
makes me wonder
if this is what Baba felt too.
If this is what it feels like
to be a celebrated cricket player.

Please, Amma

From that day onward,
Zoya insists to Amma
to let me off from all chores,
to allow me to play
because Zoya and her friends want me
on their team.
She tells Amma
(with my consent)
that I am Aarzu,
not Azlan.

Kia? asks Amma, refusing to accept,
adjusting her glasses and sizing me up.

Zoya steps in between
Amma's stern gaze and me.
It's true, Amma!
Faizan Bhai and I have known all along.

Amma purses her lips together.
I stare at my feet,
ashamed of lying.
The tip of my right foot
scratches the back of my left leg.

Amma protests to Zoya.
Want to get your amma in trouble with Barai Sahib for this?
No, no, no, no, no, no!
I will not let this happen.

Zoya holds Amma's hands in hers.
I know you'll understand.
She needs the job,
but we don't want her to work,
she practically purrs to Amma.

I can't let her off ALL chores!
Only the ones during cricket-play time,
Amma snorts.

Onward

From that day onward
> I stop wearing my dupatta
> as a turban
> while inside
> the bungalow gates.

From that day onward
> Zoya insists
> I use her bathroom
> instead of the servants' one outside.

From that day onward
> Zoya and Faizan Bhai inform everyone that I am a girl.
> The guards and servants
> call me *betiya* instead of *beta*.
> The bungalow residents make me feel like a guest
> but continue to pay me
> like I am a servant.

I feel bad for taking my whole salary
without doing all of the work,
but Zoya tells me,

You have the most important job of all.

And what is that? I ask.

Why, being on my team, of course!
She slings her arm over my shoulder.

I choke on a prayer:
Alhamdulillah.
I am so blessed to have found a job.
I am so blessed to have found Zoya.
I am so blessed to have found a way to play cricket
every day.

Nazia Doesn't

Since the day Nazia got an F on her math test, she
    doesn't sit beside me in class
    doesn't ask for help in studies
    doesn't take my book bag at home time
    doesn't speak a single word to me
    doesn't walk me to the bungalow

    doesn't inquire about Sukoon's health
    doesn't even want to be on my team when we play during
        school.

I thought she would come around,
but maybe this is how it's going to be
from now on.

I miss Nazia's

pebble-kicking,
elbow-nudging,
eyebrow-arching,
joke-cracking,
go-getting,
outsmarting,
problem-solving,
attitude-giving
attitude.

It's the kind of thing you only notice
when you don't get it anymore.

Zoya

Z- zest and zeal for cricket
O- obsessed with hashtags
Y- yanks me away from reality
A- alive—Zoya makes me feel alive again.

If Sukoon Met Zoya

I imagine them in Zoya's room
and Sukoon well enough
to be acting like her previous, curious self.

Sukoon would ogle over
Zoya's every-color nail polish collection.

Sukoon would take deep belly-breaths
of Zoya's scented diaries.

Sukoon would make funny poses
in front of Zoya's full-length mirror.

Sukoon would rub her face against Zoya's velvet cushions, repeating the words *so soft*!

Sukoon would run her fingers
over Zoya's bobblehead cat figurines and bob her own head in harmony.

While Zoya would laugh at her innocence.

Things I Teach Zoya   Things Zoya Teaches Me

Things I Teach Zoya	Things Zoya Teaches Me
How to pray	How to apply nail polish
How to bowl yorkers	How to style my short hair
How to journal	How to use chopsticks

Basant

We're taking a break
from playing cricket today
as Basant, the spring kite-flying festivities,
kicks off in Pakistan.
Dahlias, bougainvillea, pansies
bloom and blossom.
Red-eyed koels
sing spring songs.
Red, orange, yellow,
green, blue, purple
kites, the colors of hope,
catch the wind,
climb higher
up, **up, up;**
vie for height
in clear blue skies.
Kite flyers vie to win
by cutting the kite strings
of fellow contestants.
The last kite flying wins!
Mothers warn their sons:

Careful, don't trip off the roof.
The fragrance of chaat-masala-sprinkled french fries
floats out of the kitchen,
along with the scents of hot pakoras and tangy chutney,
to the garden,
where Zoya's mom and sister
draw up list upon list
of guests upon guests
and lists upon lists
of gifts upon gifts
that they plan to send out with
the wedding invites.

Faizan Bhai's tiger-striped kite
is no good in the skies.
Zoya tries
    and fails
to cheer him up
when his kite string is cut
for the fifth time in one day.

Quick Thinking

When other boys
cut Faizan Bhai's kite string,
he deflates
like a popped balloon.
His mood plummets
along with his kite,
spiraling to the ground.
If only Faizan Bhai's kite skills
were as good as
his drone-flying skills.
An idea lights my brain,
as bright as a 150-watt bulb.
That's it!
I spring up,
elbow Zoya,
and tell her my idea.

high five

Together we scurry,
drone, fallen kite, and tape in hand.
We fasten kite to drone,

take control,

lift, hover, soar.

The severed kite string matters no more!

Our laughter rises
with the kite-drone.

#GeniusAarzu
#highestkite
#tigerkite

We pose for a picture,
flashing 150-watt smiles.
Aarzu.Zoya.Faizan.

Girls' Team

As we munch on samosas,
I tell Zoya of my dreams of playing
like my baba someday.
Zoya says, *Why, what a brilliant idea!*
Let's form a girls' team,

Pakistan's first all-girls team!
I tell her that the government is running a talent-hunt program
and that the Under-15 tryouts will be in just over a month.
I tell her I've been praying that I make the team.
I tell her I've been practicing with classmates during our ghost-
    teacher periods.
I tell her how I don't know if I will get permission to play even if
    I'm selected.
What an absurd thought!
Why would anyone stop you from playing if you're selected?

> *My wishes are pinned down by reality,* I remind Zoya,
>   *like I, Aarzu, am pinned down by responsibilities.*

Tell Me More

Zoya asks me to tell her more
about Khala Ammi, Irfan, and Sukoon,
about Khaloo and Arsal.
It is almost six.
I have to rush home, I say.
Truth is, my words

will not flow easily;
this is the first time
someone has asked me, outright,
about my current family.

Back Home

When I'm done
with boiling buffalo milk for tomorrow's chai
and cleaning up after dinner
and chopping and frying the day's share of onions
and massaging Sukoon's legs
for a long time,
until she falls asleep,
I flip to the second part
in my journal and
write,
write,
write.

Khaloo

If Khaloo were to be an element
in a game of cricket, he would be a cloud.
But not just any cloud; he'd probably be a rain cloud.
Unpredictable, unwelcome, making his sudden, thundering
appearance... one you could never quite prepare for.
Dampening all the fun of the game, making everything seem hazy.
And, similar to how even the strongest stadium floodlights can
do nothing for visibility, even the best moods cannot continue
after Khaloo begins hurling his **girls-should**
and **girls-shouldn't** sermons. Like rain that lashes down,
hard and fast, spreading a damp blanket over a cricket field,
making it unfit to play, Khaloo's words leave me too soaked
to bounce back, too gloomy to stand my ground.
His very being causes my spirits to...

D
R
D   I
R   P
I   D
P   R
                     O
                     P

Arsal

If Arsal were to be an element in a game of cricket,
he would be the puddle
left behind after the rain
that poured from Khaloo, the dark rain cloud.
Even when the skies have cleared
and the game resumes,
a puddle can cause
the ball to turn
and swing in unexpected ways.
A puddle can cause a fielder or batsman
to skid and slide.
A puddle lurks,
waiting
to trap
its
next
prey.

Khala Ammi

> If Khala Ammi were to be an element in a game of cricket, she would be the third umpire. Always boxed in. Always assessing a situation closely, carefully, from every angle. Never giving her opinion unless consulted. A little distant, like a third umpire, behind a screen. A little reluctant, taking her time reaching a conclusion. But always the one to turn to for fair judgment.

Irfan

If Irfan were
to be an element in a game
of cricket, he'd be my helmet. My
trusty little helmet, always on guard,
ready to protect me from   bouncers
that Khaloo and our neighbors
hurl my way   when I want
to play.

Sukoon

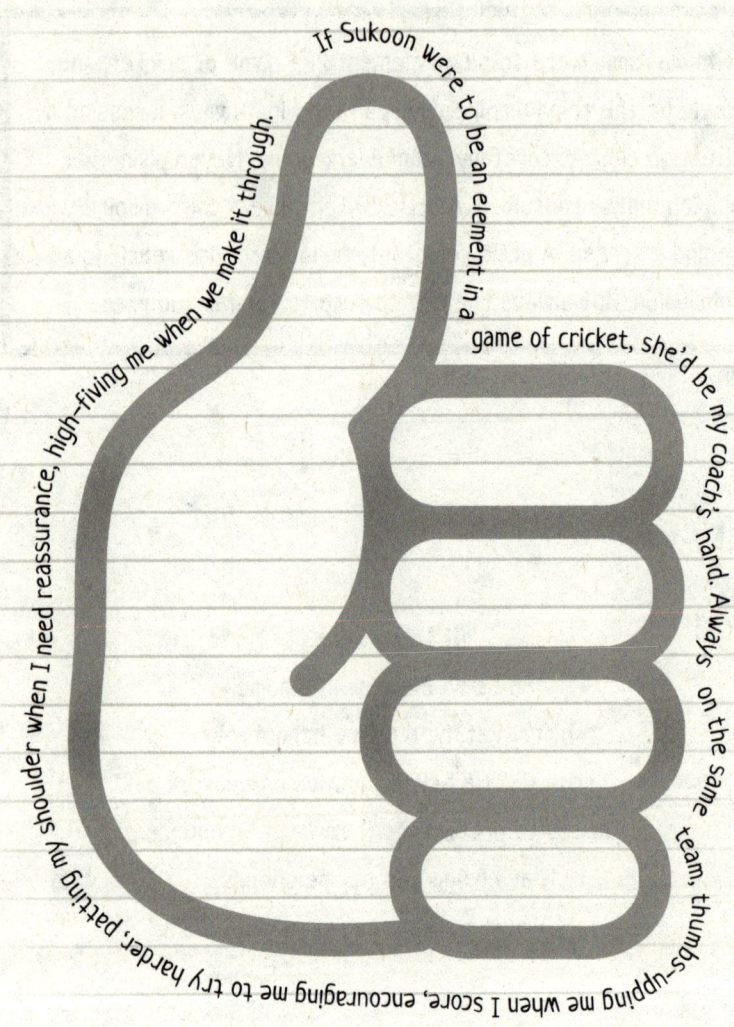

If Sukoon were to be an element in a game of cricket, she'd be my coach's hand. Always on the same team, thumbs-upping me when I score, encouraging me to try harder, patting my shoulder when I need reassurance, high-fiving me when we make it through.

Dropped

As in when a player doesn't make the team.
As in when I write Nazia's name halfway
and then scratch it out,
because why discuss a friend
who no longer speaks to you
with a friend
you're just getting to know?
Why complicate things
unnecessarily?

The next day

Zoya wipes the wetness
piling in the corners of her eyes
as she reads through my journal.
She dries my tear-streaked face
and takes my hands in hers.
We remain that way
for
what

seems

like

a

really

long

time.

When she finally speaks,
she only says, *Trip Arsal for me, will you?*
And although I'd never do such a thing,
the thought brings a smile to my face.

Uniform Design

Just for fun,
Zoya and I
sketch and design
our girls' uniform.
Zoya has set out
five shades of green nail polish
for me to pick from:
    Emerald green.
    Raw-mango green.
    Olive green.

    Guava green.
    Mehendi green.
I choose the emerald,
closest to the color of the Pakistan flag.
Zoya sketches the jersey
with short sleeves.
Beside it I sketch a version
with long sleeves
(because I do hijab. . . .
I cover everything
except my hands, wrist-downward, and face).
She adds white stripes on the track pants.
I add a golden crescent and moon on the shoulder.
Zoya designs a cap,
and I sketch a dupatta—
emerald with gold trimmings.

Identity

Why do you wear it?

                            What?

The dupatta-hijab thing, on your head?

                            Because . . .

Someone forced you?

No.

Does it feel hot?

Sometimes.

Too tight?

Sometimes.

Feel like taking it off?

No!

Why do you wear it?

What?

The cricket protective guard, around your chest?

Because . . .

Someone forced you?

No.

Does it feel hot?

Sometimes.

Too tight?

Sometimes.

Feel like taking it off?

No!
It's part of the dress code.
It makes me feel secure.
It's part of playing cricket.

Exactly!
Same with my dupatta.
It's part of MY dress code.
It makes me feel secure.
It's a part of me.

Sponsors

Faizan looks over our shoulders and says,
Shooting two birds with one stone, are we?

What's that supposed to mean?
Zoya asks what I am wondering too.
We just want to play!

Cricket is BIG money! You girls know that, right?
Companies would love to sponsor girls!
And where there's a game,
there's always prize money, too.

I don't care about being famous,
but I do care about the money I could earn from playing. . . .

It could mean Sukoon could get treated faster! Forever!
Enough so she'd never be sick again!

Gaining a sponsor
sounds like
the kind of thing
Nazia would describe as
working smart, not hard!

Are you sure? I probe further
before I get too excited.
Of course! All players are celebrities, he says,
and celebrities earn a LOT of money!

*How else do you think Imran Khan set up
the Shaukat Khanum hospital
after Pakistan won the 1992 Cricket World Cup?*

I think about Baba. . . .
I don't remember us living luxurious lives,
but I do remember us being better off than our neighbors,
and I know Khaloo keeps prodding Khala Ammi
about why we haven't been able to get our hands on Baba's
    savings.

Plus, there's prize money if you win games. . . .

Zoya looks at me,
I look at Zoya,
and we both mouth,
"Sukoon!"

The Pakistani Flag

Our flag is green
with a white strip
and a white crescent
and a white star.
Green is the color of Islam
and represents the majority Muslim population.
White is for minorities.
In Zoya's home I am the minority.
In Zoya's home I am the white.

But Zoya's household
makes me feel special . . .
a necessary part
to complete the whole.

Unpredictable

As in a player whose performance cannot be predicted during a game.

As in how Sukoon will feel and behave on any given day.

On good days Sukoon's symptoms are manageable:
>fatigue
>
>nausea
>
>slight swelling.

On bad days Sukoon struggles with
>extreme lethargy
>
>vomiting
>
>unbearable pain (especially when using the bathroom)
>
>and a lot of swelling.

Sister Time

One evening I skip home
with a bottle of emerald nail polish
that Zoya gifted me.
After dinner I sit Sukoon down on our mattress.
Lie back and relax, I instruct her.
She looks slightly less swollen,
a good day.
Maybe the dialysis is working.
She giggles and asks, *What's up, Aaru Aapi?*
Wait and watch, I say.
Or rather, close your eyes.

I take a small towel and soak it in water.
I dab it on her eyes.
Fancy people call this a spa, Suki!

Aspa? she asks.
No, no, spa! I say. *Just* spa!

She repeats the word *spa*, slowly parting her lips
like she does when she blows spit bubbles.

Spread your fingers, and don't fidget! I instruct.

Sukoon giggles as the cold coats of polish tingle her fingers.
Her fascination reminds me of
my awe at the sights and sounds
the first time I stepped into the bungalow.

She takes a belly-breath. *Aah, this smells so good, Aapi.*

It does! I say.
It smells of freedom.

The Power of Politicians

Zoya tells her da'eee
about the national Under-15 girls cricket team,
for which there will be tryouts
happening at my school
and all over Pakistan.
And within a couple of days,
she has "made" the team

(and by extension, so have I)
because her da'eee
has acquired approval
in writing from authorities,
politician friends,
who are powerful,
just like him.
Nazia's words
(that I dismissed as an exaggeration)
echo in my ears:
The family is mighty powerful
and very influential.
Sahib is a politician—
he has connections right to the top!

An ex-player has volunteered
to coach us girls
starting a week after the wedding is over.
If the sponsorship makes us money,
like Faizan Bhai says it will,
I will soon be able to earn
by doing what I love.
And for the first time ever
my passion for cricket

won't make me feel selfish,
because it will help me
fulfill my responsibility
toward Sukoon.

Transplant

When I get home,
I hear Sukoon's moans
even before I enter the house.
As she sees me, Khala Ammi taps the stool beside her.
Aaru, sit.
You know it's been a month
since Sukoon started receiving
dialysis treatment.
It seemed like it was working.
Khala Ammi puts her tired hands around my shoulders.
But do you know what the doctor said today?
I look down at my feet,
scratch the back of my left leg
with the tip of my right foot.
I shake my head,

too scared to think.
Sukoon doesn't look good, I say.
That's right. We need to collect
more money
and find a match
for Sukoon.
A kidney donor.
A transplant is
our last hope.
Till we do find a donor
and collect the money,
Sukoon will need to receive dialysis
more often . . . thrice a week.
I realize that
the sponsors
and possible gift money
are going to
be needed soon,
very soon.
But I don't tell Khala Ammi
my plan just yet . . .
because that would mean
I'd also have to tell her
about my hair

and job at the bungalow
and all the other things
I've been hiding from her.
I think the weight of my betrayal of her trust
will surely outweigh the relief she may feel
if I tell her I have it all figured out.

Hang in There

When I enter our room,
I see Sukoon
clutching,
unclutching her thighs.
I feel her pain
in my thighs
and fall onto my knees
beside her.
My little warrior,
your Aaru Aapi has a plan.
I have been collecting money.
Shh, don't tell anyone. . . .
I lift my long dupatta from the milk crate in which I store my clothes

and unwrap the bat-doodled gullak.
I rub it like Aladdin rubs his magic lamp
for the wish-granting genie to appear.
I'm not sure if Sukoon is hearing what I'm saying,
but I continue anyway.
Soon we'll have enough money
to get you the treatment you need.
You have to be strong.
Just a while longer.
I take her swollen fingers
in the palms of my hands
and squeeze them gently,
careful not to hurt her.
I choke on my tears.
My hands say the words
my lips do not utter:
Hang in there!
Sukoon squeezes back:
Thank you.

The Right Way

Even though I have "made" the team,
it doesn't feel like the right way to do things.
When it is time for tryouts at school,
I will turn up
to show the selectors what I've got.
It's the Right Way to do it.
And MamaBaba taught me that
the right way is the
ONLY way.

Spinning

When rains lash Karachi's streets for the first time this year, I am at the bungalow. Zoya and I race each other to the garden, stretch out our hands out to our sides, forming Ts.

We spin around and around and around again, with limitless energy, faster and faster. We laugh for no reason . . . harder and harder and harder still.

Until we

fall to the ground,

doubled over,

clutching our sides

that ache from all the laughing.

When I'm at Zoya's,

all the worries I carry

seem to wash away

like dust and dirt wash away

from buildings and trees,

leaving everything looking

fresh after Mother

Nature's

shower.

Dragonflies

Swarms of dragonflies
descend on Karachi after
the rains. Their green color reminds me of the
color of my jersey-to-be, which reminds me of the
girls' team, which reminds me of my cropped hair, which
reminds me of all the lies I continue to tell Khala
Ammi.
The dragonflies make me feel
like my stomach is filled with dragons blowing
fire. It's funny how just a color can make me feel so hopeful
and guilty all at once. But I don't mind it, because this
is the only chance I have to get Sukoon

the

treatment

she

needs.

Even

if

the

medication

and

treatments

sometimes make her barf,
they're getting her closer to living a
healthy life. So I'll take all the dragonflies
if it means everything is eventually going to get
better. And soon I won't have to hide from Khala Ammi,
or Irfan, or Sukoon. Maybe Khala Ammi
won't
be upset when she sees
how much I've earned. When she sees the amount
I've collected, she will agree that this was my only
chance to earn enough for Sukoon's treatment. And,
InshAllah, soon I will be living my dream
guilt-free,
with
all
the
people
I
love
cheering
me
on.

T – 5 Days to the Wedding

The ghazal singers
arrive to set up their stage
and their instruments
in the basement
of Zoya's house.
I race through my chores
to join Zoya and Faizan Bhai downstairs.
This will be the first of many functions
that lead up to the final rukhsati event,
when the bride will leave
for her husband's home.
Zoya, Faizan Bhai, and I
take a gol takiya each,
tuck them behind our backs,
and recline like royalty,
drumming our fingers to
the melancholy melody
as the ghazal singers check their microphones.

#Napkin_Ghazal

Let's write our own ghazal, I whisper to Zoya.
I scribble a couplet on a napkin
and pass it to Zoya:

Won't you come see us play and support us, cricket girls?
Whacking fours and sixes, wicket-taking cricket girls!

She adds her lines:
#CrescentStar logos, white-striped, emerald-green tracks,
#dupattas&braids tied in place, we're in our cricket gear, girls.

Zoya passes it back to me:
Rain clouds 'ave parted, weather forecast's clear.
Bring out the banners! Time to cheer, GO, GREEN! GO, GIRLS!

Slap on sunscreen, bring some sodas, we hope to inspire.
Helmets on, pads in place! Come witness us on fire, girls!

We'll take selfies, tagged #GirlsinGreen #playcricket.
History's waiting to witness a score for cricket, girls!

I save the napkin to tape into my journal
after Zoya takes a picture and posts it to her socials.

It would also make for the perfect addition,
    another hope,
    another dream,
    another framed napkin
    to hang on my imaginary room wall.

T – 1 Day to the Wedding

When the henna ladies come
with their henna cones and design catalogues,
the women of the house,
family, friends, and acquaintances gather
for the pre-wedding tradition
of painting paisleys and flowery vines,
like tattooed lace gloves
all the way to their elbows.
Zoya and I rush to get our palms decorated
before the clock strikes six.
But we do not choose a pattern from their catalogue.
We've already decided on exactly what we want. . . .

Stained Hands II

My hands
stained with henna
will tell a story of a shared secret
between me and Zoya
and the love we share for cricket.
Three lines
on our middle fingers
form the wickets.
A large circle
on our palms
will form the cork ball.
Zoya and Aarzu,
Aarzu and Zoya.
I'll hold my hands up
before I head home.
My palms wet with henna
will face the skies
to praise Allah
like you taught me to,
MamaBaba.

Informed

On my way home I
scratch
scratch
scratch
at the now dried scabs of henna.
The stain has sunk
d
e
e
p
into the layers of my skin.
How could I have been so silly?
How am I going to explain
hennaed hands to Khala Ammi?
But when I enter our lane
and catch a glimpse of Khala Ammi
at the entrance
of our building,
her gaze piercing me
despite the distance between us,
I swallow a
cork-ball-sized lump

that forms in my throat.
I want to take
                two steps
    back
                      for every step
                              I take forward.
I guess explaining my hennaed hands
will be the least of my concerns.
Khala Ammi has been informed
of I'm-not-sure-what.
But I'm sure of one thing:
I've been played.

Partnership Broken

Icanexplain, are the first words that tumble clumsily out of my
   mouth
as I catch my breath when I am close enough
for Khala Ammi to hear.
Before hearing what Khala Ammi might've wanted to say,
I've cornered myself into a fix—
where I've confirmed my guilt
even before I've heard her concerns.

Khal . . . , I start off, and choke on my words
when I see Khaloo glaring down
from the balcony above.
Even from down here
I can tell from his eyeballs,
ready to plunge from their sockets,
that his anger is through the roof.

Large sweat beads,
the size of coriander seeds,
speckle Khala Ammi's upper lip.
She squeezes her eyes together,
swallows hard, and raises her hand
as if taking an oath never to trust me again.
I clutch my dupatta pullos
to steady my quivering hands
and hide the henna stain.

My legs want to run me back to the bungalow,
but that could get me into even more trouble.

I trudge up the stairs behind Khala Ammi,
not two at a time like I usually do.

Left.
 Right.
Left.
 Right.
Left.
 Right.
 All the way to the top.
 I will my feet
 to carry me to my room
 to carry me to my doom.

Golden Duck

As in when a batsman gets out on the first ball.
As in when I have a long list of excuses
to tell Khala Ammi
 why I was afraid to confide in her,
 why I hid all my dreams and hopes from her,
 why I thought her knowing would mean more trouble for us
  both
 why I broke her trust when she trusted me so.
Her silence when she raises her hand

every time I open my mouth
to stop my words in their tracks
carries her message
loud and clear:
NO EXCUSE WILL BE GOOD ENOUGH!

Just like no explanation from a batsman
who gets out on a golden duck
is good enough to justify
his place on the team,
I guess no explanation from me
will be good enough to justify
my lies.

Arsal smirks

and mouths the word *NAZIA*
as tears sting my eyes.
If anyone had friends like yours,
they wouldn't need enemies!
She told Mama what you've been hiding.
Tch. Tch. Tch. He sucks at his front teeth.

There is an Urdu proverb that says,
Tough times test friendships.

I knew Nazia was failing tests at school.
But now I know Nazia has failed me,
and our friendship, too.

Khaloo Jeers

*See how your dutiful niece
has deceived you?
This is what happens
when you allow girls
outdoors alone!
The news has spread
throughout the neighborhood
like wildfire. . . .*
I cower at our room door,
my head bowed in shame.
He stomps and spits
as he thunders past me.

I notice how
he doesn't refer to me
by my name.

I guess it makes it easier
to say hurtful things
to a nobody.

Irfan Sobs

We searched all over for you!
Aaru Aapi, Alhamdulillah, you're okay!
He makes sure Khaloo is out of the house
before he wraps his arms around my waist
and locks his fingers behind my back.

Sukoon says

nothing.
She wakes from a deep sleep and
pats her pillow,
signaling for me to lie close.
Her little hands
and her frail legs
wrap around me
like a warm blanket
on a stormy night.

I wish . . .

Khala Ammi had a totka
to fix this mess
I find myself in.
I don't even know what Khala Ammi knows.
>	Does she know where I went?
>	Does she know why I went?
>	What all did Nazia tell her?

Why did Nazia tell her?
When did Nazia tell her?
Did Nazia come over especially to tell her?

Suspended

As in when a player is made to sit out a match due to breaking the rules.
As in when I am not allowed to go anywhere:
- No cricket.
- No school.
- No meeting Nazia.
- No bungalow.
- No seeing Zoya.
- No selling onions myself at the bazaar.
- No grocery trips to the bazaar with Khala Ammi.

The only things I am allowed to do are:
- Onion chopping.
- Onion frying.
- Onion packing.

The things I have to do more of are:
- Roti-making.
- Dish washing.
- House sweeping.
- Furniture dusting.
- Clothes washing.
- Laundry folding.
- Clothes ironing.

Detention Lines

I will never trust Nazia again.
I will never trust Nazia again.
I will never trust Nazia again.
I will never trust Nazia again.
I will never trust Nazia again.
I will never trust Nazia again.
I will never trust Nazia again.
I will never trust Nazia again.
I will never trust Nazia again.
I will never trust Nazia again.
I will never trust Nazia again.
I will never trust Nazia again.
I will never trust Nazia again.
I will never trust Nazia again.
I will never trust Nazia again.
I will never trust Nazia again.
I will never trust Nazia again.
I will never trust Nazia again.
I will never trust Nazia again.
I will never trust Nazia again.
I will never trust Nazia again.
I will never trust Nazia. Period.

The next morning

when Khaloo leaves to drop Arsal off at school,
I twist and turn my hennaed hands
as if I am still wringing wet clothes.
Excuses form in my head
but >pOp< like soapy bubbles
on their way out.
I open my mouth,
but it produces no words.
No explanation.
No apology.
Nothing.
I feel small
for not confiding in Khala Ammi.
Not even me? Aaru?
You didn't EVEN trust ME?
Khala Ammi keeps repeating in Mama's voice,
between sobs and sabzi-cooking.
Why does she have to sound
exactly like Mama
when she is upset?
It breaks me
even more.

When I turn to Sukoon,
for comfort and maybe a cuddle,
she snorts and turns over to her side.
But I can explain . . . , I murmur-protest.
Sukoon turns around,
looks me straight in the eyes,
and then rolls hers 360 degrees.
When did she learn to do that?

Maiden

As in when a bowler bowls an entire over,
six balls,
without a batsman managing to score even a single run.
As in when it's been six days
and I haven't found the words
to explain my actions
or apologize to Khala Ammi.
~~I'm sure~~ I've missed so much work at school,
Zoya's sister is probably married,
and I've missed the official tryouts.
I want to break this dot ball streak
so bad.

Know?

I wonder what Nazia has told my teachers and classmates.
Would she have told everyone what she told Khala Ammi?
What must my cricket mates
Mariam, Tahira, Zeenat, and Ismat
be thinking about my disappearance?
Haven't my classmates wondered where I've gone?
Or wondered why a star player wouldn't turn up for tryouts?
Or wondered why a star student would miss so many days of school?
And if they have, why haven't they come looking for me?

Creases I Want to X

Mama,
just like you used to,
I now iron every piece
of clothing
in the house …
from underpants to socks,
from shalwar kameezs and dupattas

to the white knitted caps
Khaloo and the boys wear
for prayers.
I view the creases
on the clothes I've laundered
as fault lines,
like those created
after a violent quake.
A quake that swallowed you
and Baba whole.

I like cranking up the heat
like you used to, Mama,
focusing
on one crease at a time,
making sure I trace an *X* with the iron
over and over,
until the creases shrink,
until the cloth eases.
But some creases
refuse to ease—
like the gashes
in our hearts
after you and Baba left.

All the love
and warmth
from Khala Ammi
has not been enough
to ease the pain.
And now I've made it even worse
by losing the trust of your only sister, Mama.

Creases I Don't Want to X

But there is one crease
that I love...
just like you used to,
Baba.
Its image
flashes before me,
awake
or asleep.
I dream
of the cricket crease—
those two lines on a cleared patch
of land

at the center
of the stadium.
I never want anyone
to X this crease
out of my life.
Despite my name,
and your prayers for me,
it doesn't seem like
any of my wishes are coming true,
MamaBaba.

Pretend Play

The worst part about not being allowed outside
is not being able to play cricket.
After I finish my chores,
while I pretend to bathe
in the bathroom for nearly an hour,
I stand diagonally
to allow myself maximum space
to throw back and swing my bowling arm.
My fingers release an imaginary ball.

Sometimes I hold the bathroom wiper,
pretending it is my bat.
I adjust the distance between my hands,
making sure my grip feels right.
Like a batswoman taking in the field arrangement,
I look at the bare bulb on the wall,
the chipped mirror side,
the latch on the door,
the frayed curtains on the mini window,
imagining they are
Mariam, Tahira, Zeenat, Ismat,
my school seniors, fielding as I bat.

When I wash clothes,
I sneak one of Arsal's tennis balls into the bathroom,
layer a towel at the bottom of the bucket
(so the ball makes no noise upon contact),
and practice my aim,
so I am a better fielder
once I return to the field.

Seven

It's been seven days that I haven't
stepped out of the house,
but it sure does
feel like

INFINITY.

If everything had gone
according to plan,
today would have been the day
that our cricket coaching
would've begun.
Today would've been the day
we'd be one step closer to Sukoon's transplant.
I wonder what Zoya
must think of my disappearance.
I wonder if she misses me
as much as I miss her.

Sister Joke

The only thing that keeps me going
is spending more time around Sukoon.
It makes me think of happy days,
before Sukoon's illness,
before our move to Karachi,
before we were separated from MamaBaba.

Since Sukoon was a baby,
I've been her entertainer.
It's not like I ever had to try;
I would raise my hand,
       and she would laugh.
I would sneeze,
       and she would laugh.
I would fart,
       and she would laugh.

As she grew older,
she only laughed when I did things in
an extra jerky, bumpy, bouncy way.

When she'd be fussing
about her mashed khichri
with pursed lips,
I'd pretend to dramatically drop her bowl
of mushy rice, lentils, potatoes, peas,
and she'd break into a laugh.

I'd seize the opportunity
to smuggle a bite into her,
and then do it all over again
for her next bite.
When I see Sukoon
being fussy about eating,
I tell her of these tactics,
and just like when we were little,
she breaks into a laugh
and I'm able to feed her
a few morsels.

Selected

As in when a player is chosen for the squad.
As in when Khala Ammi finally selects me, over Arsal,
to accompany her to the bazaar
to help carry the weight
of the weekly groceries.
Stepping out feels like I'm a mole
coming out of a hole.
The rickshaws puff their black smoke.
The bus drivers blare their loud music.
The street vendors holler their rates.
Fruit pyramids on thellas lure customers.
Toddlers whine for sweet jalebis,
and the Karachi sun makes everything
appear brighter and louder.
But, unlike a mole, I relish all
the sights and sounds
of the bustling street bazaars.
Until . . .
halfway to the market
we turn a corner and I catch a glimpse
of fresh graffiti on the wall . . .
I freeze.

> **NO CRICKET FOR GIRLS**
> **GOOD GIRLS STAY HOME**
> **GOOD GIRLS PLAY INDOORS**
> **GOOD GIRLS SLAY TEMPTATION**

Khala Ammi sees

what I see

and clasps my arm,

pulls me into gear

like the rickshaw driver down the street.

March, she commands.

I do as I am told.

But the writing on the wall

lodges a lump in my throat

like I've swallowed another cork ball.

Anger blisters my insides

worse than scorching concrete

would blister bare feet.

The wetness of my eyes

blurs all the brightness of the outdoors.

The lup-DUPP, lup-DUPP of my heart

drowns out the sounds swirling around me.

Like a flashlight switched on in the darkness,
a plan forms in my head,
showing me the way forward.
At the bazaar
I remind Khala Ammi
that Arsal is out of ink
for his fountain pens.
We get a kilo of basmati rice,
two liters each of milk and oil,
three kilos of aata flour,
six kilos of onions,
a pot of ink,
and head back home.
I shift the weight of the plastic bags
to my right hand,
unscrew the pot of ink with my left. . . .

    SPLASH

    SPLASH   SPLASH

    SPLASH   SPLASH

    SPLASH   SPLASH

        DASH!

Double Penalty

I do not wait to see
how Khala Ammi responds—
I already know
I've let her down yet AGAIN.
She may never let me
accompany her to the bazaar again.
She may never let me step out again.
She may never, ever trust me again.
But even so,
sending this message
was worth it!

Rain

After our bazaar trip
Khala Ammi sends
Arsal, Irfan, and me
to the rooftop
to collect the laundry
from the clotheslines
as soon as we hear
the thundering clouds.
By the time we hop over
the TV antennae and cables
on the rooftop of our building,
everything, including us, is already drenched.
Splat. Splot. Splotch.
We wade through.
Irfan and I pluck the kameezes and shalwars
and pile them into the growing load
in Arsal's arms.
Jao, jao, before they get even more wet!
I instruct Arsal to hurry down.
He grunts as he wades toward the stairs.
I look over the masjid minarets
in the direction of my school

and spot Zoya and Faizan Bhai's ivory home
standing out amongst the earthen slum buildings.
Lightning crackles.
Irfan clutches my dupatta corner and tugs.
Chalo! Aaru Aapi, it's scary up here.
My dupatta slips,
exposing my shabbily cropped hair.
Arsal gasps as if he's seen a ghost.
He dumps the drenched laundry
(Twerp!)
and races down.
I race after him,
before I realize
Irfan isn't following us.
I run back up to find a frozen Irfan
and a pile of now muddy, wet clothes.

Inspection

Khala Ammi's face is as white as a ghost
when I reach downstairs.
She pulls me in,
spins me around

and around,
inspecting me
and my cropped hair
like one would survey
the broken blades of a fan.

Is Aaru Aapi a boy?
Irfan's sobbing, confused words interrupt
Khala Ammi's scrutinizing gaze.
Great! Now Khala Ammi probably thinks that,
along with being a liar,
and selfish,
and irresponsible
(for wanting to play when there is so much to worry about),
I also want to be a boy!

Her face is hollow of emotion.
I look down at my feet,
scratch the back of my left shin
with the tip of my right foot.
She signals to me to vanish into my room.

I want to tell Khala Ammi
why . . .

when . . .
how . . .
where . . .
what . . .
about my cropped hair
and all that I've been keeping a secret.
I want it all to spill out,
but her eyes squeeze together;
she swallows hard and raises her hand.
My words, halfway out,
weigh me down,
heavier than my drenched dupatta
hanging on my shoulders.
Nazia gave me the worst advice.
It is NOT easier to ask for forgiveness.
I should've known better than to trust her.
I should've asked for permission.
I should've confided in Khala Ammi,
rather than Nazia.

Actions Are Judged by Intentions

is an essential Islamic belief
that gives me hope.
I have to tell Khala Ammi that my intentions were clear.
I wasn't going to the bungalow to play.
I wasn't going to the bungalow to run away from my
    responsibility toward Sukoon.
I wasn't going to the bungalow to make friends and have a good
    time.

My sole intention
in cutting my locks
was to look like a boy
to get the job
at the bungalow.

My sole intention
in getting the job
was to earn ALL the money
to fund Sukoon's treatment
and not be a burden
on Khala Ammi.

My sole intention
in hiding from Khala Ammi
was so that she wouldn't have to worry about me.
Since she didn't know what I was up to,
she wouldn't get in trouble
with Khaloo
if things somehow got messed up.

My sole intention
in continuing to hide from Khala Ammi
was so that I could collect
the entire amount
needed for Sukoon's surgery.

Sujood

Muslims believe
that when you bend low
into sujood,
your forehead touching the floor,
a state of complete submission to Allah,
your whispered duas soar.
They resound in the heavens
and are answered
faster.

I stay in sajdah longer.
And plead to Allah for forgiveness
and plead to Allah to help me find a way
to plead to Khala Ammi for forgiveness.

Locked Words

When I write in my diary,
my words f
        l
           o
              w with ease.
When I batted,
                                       y
                                   l
                        my strokes would f
with ease.
But when I try
to speak to Khala Ammi,
I line up my words,
like ducks in a row,
into short, concise sentences, then push
                        PUSH
                              PUSH my words,
and yet they scatter,
like ducklings,
as if they've forgotten
the way to my tongue.

They
remain
locked
deep
within
me.

I_Will_NOT_Blend_In

Khala Ammi hands me a tray
with condiments and a steaming bowl
of chaat-masala-sprinkled haleem in our room.
A broth mix of six types of lentils
pounded, swirled, masked with spices,
reduced to a single, seamless mass,
much like our family of six,
shrouded in
the color of Khaloo's
faulty beliefs.
I squeeze a lemon
over my haleem,
pulp, juice, seeds, and all.
I add fried onions,
sliced raw ginger, and green chilies.
I want to speak out,
stand out,
like the seeds, ginger, and onions,
that do not blend in,
sharp and pungent
in my haleem broth.

I want to announce:
I WILL NOT BLEND IN!
Instead I tear a piece of tandoor naan,
dunk it into the haleem, and
stuff
bite
upon
bite
until my mouth can hold no more.
Swallow! I command myself.

A single, seamless mass,
naan, haleem, lemon seeds, onions, ginger,
mixes with everything else swirling within me:
anger
hope
identity
words.
Sharp. Sour. Pungent. Hot.

Visit to the Mangroves

Arsal's science teacher
takes his students,
his *private* school students,
to visit the mangrove plantations
along the strip of Arabian Sea
that kisses Karachi's coast:
Sandspit and Hawke's Bay.
I can't wait to hear all about it.
Arsal convinces Khala Ammi
to allow him to take her phone
to snap some pictures
and record audios
of his teacher speaking
so I can help him
with the assignment that will follow.
I wish it was me going to the mangroves,
but since I go to public school,
we never have field trips,
and even if we did,
Khaloo wouldn't let me go,
so this seems like the next best thing.

Questions and Answers

Arsal's mangrove assignment is due at the end of the week.

Based on your trip to the mangrove plantation, answer the questions below:

Q1. What are mangroves?
Q2. What hostile environment do they thrive in?
Q3. How have these plants developed special features to help them cope in this environment?

I dictate the answers to Arsal:

A1. Mangroves are shrubs that line coastal regions.
A2. Mangroves thrive in salty seawater.
A3. Their special roots stick out of the water, like straws, for breathing.

He writes the answers down
word
for
word,
and all the while
I'm waiting for him to finish,

I twist and turn Arsal's assignment
in my head.
> *Hostile environment.*
> *Special roots.*
> *Thrive.*

Sukoon yelps in discomfort.
How are we going to get her the transplant
if I continue to stay silent?
Somewhere in my head
a light bulb flickers....
Nazia's words ring out:
You are tougher than you think!
The muscles around my lips contort
as if salt water has made them taut.
This sticky situation is the salty seawater through which
I have to find a way to thrive.
The voice inside my head, soft but firm, whispers,
Time to toughen up, Aarzu!
This game isn't over yet.
I need to find the answers,
and my voice.
I need to devise
my own straw solution.

Lessons from Islam

I begin scanning Qur'an translations.
I pray for guidance in the words of Allah.
I flip through my Islamic Studies books.
I need to fortify myself
for the storm brewing within me.
I learn the dua of Prophet Musa
from the Qur'an:
"... *make my task easy for me*
and untie the knot in my tongue...."
I repeat it over and over
till my hands do not tremble
and my head does not swirl
at the thought of speaking out.
I need to refresh my memory
of stories from Islamic history,
of the strong, virtuous ladies
who thrived in hostile environments,
who achieved great things
in an era much tougher on women than ours is.

Lady Khadijah, wife of Prophet Muhammad (peace be upon him),

businesswoman
owner of fancy trade caravans
in male-dominated ancient Arabia.

Lady Asiya, adoptive mother of Prophet Musa,
who protected and nurtured him,
defying orders from Pharoah,
her tyrannical husband.

Lady Zaynab, granddaughter of Prophet Muhammad
(peace be upon him),
who spoke against her oppressors
while chained in captivity,
in a court full of men.

These stories move something within me.
Women are NOT weak.
Women are NOT unable.
Women were NOT born to be oppressed.
Women are NOT meant to be treated the way we are.
Women are meant to be respected
the way Prophet Muhammad
(peace be upon him)
respected his daughter Lady Fatimah

(peace be upon her).
I was so wrong in trying to prove
I can be as good as a boy.

Culture Is the Culprit

So if it isn't Islam
that stops women
from reaching their potential,
then the culprit has to be our culture!
Disguising itself
behind the veil of religion.
Making the veil
we women wear
appear debilitating, limiting,
when it is the very thing
that makes me feel free and liberated.

Gol Rotis

Sukoon's condition is
worsening day by day, hour by hour.
With the strength of Khadijah, the defiance
of Asiya, the eloquence of Zaynab, and the dua of
Prophet Musa, I will tell Khala Ammi about my
secret plan to raise funds for Sukoon's surgery. When
she knows, she will be so proud! But how will she know
if she leaves the room every time I open my mouth to
offer an apology, to clarify my intentions? But today I
have a plan! I will make the roundest rotis Khala
Ammi has ever seen. When she sees them, she
will gasp with surprise. Her mouth
will fall open for sure!

Not that I care for gol
rotis, but I will make them just the
way she does, to show her I never intended
to be a rebel. Only, I need to cheat to get them
perfectly circular. I roll the dough in whatever shape
I roll it, and place a quarter plate upside down over it. I
trace along its edges with a knife, to get a perfect circle.
When Khala Ammi comes to the kitchen after her
shower, I have a stack of round rotis, the most perfect
stack of the roundest rotis. Her mouth forms an O.
Her dimple dances on her left cheek. Her
arms encircle me. Warm gol rotis
finally break the ice!

Enough

That glimpse of Khala Ammi's dimple is enough
for me to confide in her.
She is in Mama's place.
Even though I've kept silent,
even though I've lied,
even though I haven't trusted her,
despite her trusting me,
she will understand,
just like a mother always does.
She will take me back
under her wing.
Khala Ammi will accept me, and my apology, too.
Besides, she deserves to know
the truth—the whole truth.
And why I was doing
what I was doing.
And now, now is the time
to share my plans with her.

Bouncing Back

Before I can tell Khala Ammi everything,
Bano Aunty's son
comes to drop off the earnings
from the fried onions
he sells on my behalf
at the weekly Mangal Bazaar
(since I've been grounded).
He tells me, *Your friend came again this week.*
I think she misses you.
Who? I ask.
Bano Aunty's son scratches his head.
I think she said Nadia, *but I'm not sure.*
Nazia! Khala Ammi says over my shoulder.
Yes, maybe. Yes, Aunty, you're probably right.
She is always the last customer.
And she always buys whatever of your stock is left!
I didn't know that! I say with a smile.
I take the money and thank him,
but inside I'm seething with anger.
Backstabber, I swear under my breath.
Nazia isn't a backstabber, Aaru!

What made you say that?
Khala Ammi asks.
Best friends don't tell on you! I grunt.
She didn't really tell on you.
I came looking for you
when Sukoon's health suddenly deteriorated
and she kept asking for you and crying.
When we didn't find you at school,
I went to Nazia's.
She told me I could find you at the bungalow.
I was in such a frenzy, she had to let me know!
Did Nazia tell you I play cricket there too? I ask.
No way! Khaloo got a call from your school
about some cricket tryouts.
We had no clue about the bungalow, nor about the tryouts.
But we found out about both together
and assumed you went to the bungalow to play cricket!

Confide

I tell her I'm ashamed.
I tell her I'm sorry.

I tell her I wasn't running from my responsibilities.

I tell her I cut my hair to get a job at the bungalow.

I tell her I was at the bungalow to earn money to fund Sukoon's transplant.

I tell her playing was just what I did when I was done with my chores.

I tell her how I practiced at school and at the bungalow whenever I got the chance.

Khala Ammi Understands

Sukoon's not doing too good, she says.
The doctor said she doesn't have a chance
without the transplant. . . .
Aaru beti, there's no time to dillydally.
I would've sold more jewelry if I had any remaining.

Khala Ammi pulls her dupatta back
to reveal a fresh purple bruise.
My wide eyes are question marks.
My blinking eyelids are exclamation points.
It all makes sense. . . .

Khala Ammi sneaking out on Sundays,
stuffing pouches under her kurta.
That's probably where the money for Sukoon's
many in-between appointments and medications came from.

Khala Ammi continues . . .
Khaloo sold most of my jewelry to pay the apartment rent
that he hasn't been paying for months.
He loses his temper when he finds out
I've sold gold trinkets
to pay for Sukoon's treatment.
But now I have none left,
and Khaloo is barely making anything
driving his rickshaw.
Even if he does,
Sukoon's treatment is not a priority for him.
But you girls are my responsibility.
I don't know how we will carry on. . . .
She chokes on her words.

Tears sting my eyes.
We've both been working so hard
to keep secrets from each other
and we've both been working so hard

doing whatever we can
to earn for Sukoon's treatments.

We sit together for what seems like hours,
as I stroke her back, up and down, up and down,
until finally her uncontainable sobs
give way to a looong sigh.

"Back in the Game" . . .

is the feeling I get
when Khala Ammi holds me close.
When she finally stops weeping,
I explain to her,
We can now consider
having the transplant.
I tell her how disguising myself as a boy was necessary
to get out of the house
to do the things
I thought
only boys can do.
I tell her

I've realized since then that
I do not need to compare
myself to anyone,
especially not to a boy!

Surprise Parcel

Khala Ammi rises to her feet
when our doorbell rings a second time.
Who could it be?
We never have visitors
unless it's a neighbor
asking for a cup of sugar
or a few tablespoons of ghee.
Khala Ammi gets the door before I do
and receives a parcel.
Without asking whom it is from,
she quickly re-latches the door,
probably afraid the neighbors will catch a glimpse
and report the big red boxed parcel to Khaloo.
She unpacks the parcel rather clumsily.
She holds up an emerald-green jersey,

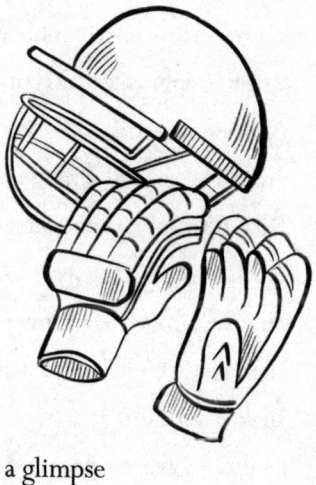

flips it over to witness

my name glistening in gold.

I bite my lip, and hold back my excitement,

thinking the jersey will spark

memories of my betrayal and lies.

But Khala Ammi continues unwrapping the parcel.

A gold crescent and star

glow on white-striped track pants.

Pakola soda and Igloo ice cream logos

flash from the uniform.

A wooden cricket bat

with a crimson-red rubber grip boasts

a neatly engraved Pakistan flag.

A green dupatta

etched with gold piping unravels.

Khala Ammi lays the jersey flat

on the dining table,

runs her fingers over my name,

then holds it closetoherheart and

shakes her head

s l o w l y from side to side,

which either means

I-remember-your-dream

or *I-cannot-believe-this* (in a good way?!).

Her dimple sneaks up onto her left cheek
before she catches it and hides it away,
and I know she remembers
and I know we are back on the same team.
She finally tosses the jersey and tracks my way,
    throws the wall clock a glance, and
        signals to me with the flick of her brows
            to have the stuff hidden before Arsal comes home.
I go to bury the uniform
at the very bottom of my clothes box,
to keep it safe from the stench of fried onions.
That's when I find . . .

A Note

Aarzu,
where'd you disappear?
Anything we can do to help?
ANYTHING?
We're here if you need us.
Please come back!
Zoya and Faizan Bhai

P. S: We remembered your apartment from the day we flew the drone over your building.

P. P. S: Isn't the jersey the coolest ever? Can't wait for you to join practice with Coach.

I empty my milk crate

so I can bury my cricket gear
and fetch my bat-doodled gullak
to quickly show Khala Ammi
how much money
I have been saving
from the bungalow salary
for Sukoon's surgery.

Absent hurt,

as in when a player gets so severely hurt
during a game that he (or she) is unable to play further.
As in when I find that my gullak,
the one with the bat doodle,
has already been broken into.
Only shards of terra-cotta clay
are strewn where my bungalow-salary gullak once lay.
I feel like someone has slit my gut
with each of the broken shards.
I carry them in my dupatta to Khala Ammi
and tell her I think it must be Arsal
who did the deed
while I took one of my long showers.
Khala Ammi holds her head between her hands.
Her shoulders jolt violently.
I'm sorry. I'm so, so sorry, Aaru.
Sukoon shuffles out of our room
looking weaker than ever
and comes to witness
what all the commotion is about.

Team Huddle

Khala Ammi embraces us:
puts her right arm around me,
puts her left arm around Sukoon,
and pulls us in for a huddle hug.
We'll get through this, I whisper,
wiping their tears with the edge of my dupatta.
Time to toughen up!

What Will People Say?

When I explain to Khala Ammi how
my passion for cricket
can help us in our struggle to save Sukoon,
she understands perfectly.

But she trembles thinking about
> what Khaloo will say,
> what the neighbors will say,
> what society will say.

They won't understand our intentions, Aaru!
They won't! They won't! They won't. . . .
Didn't you see the writing on the wall?
Khala Ammi is inconsolable.
Until I share the stories
of Khadija, Aasiya, and Zaynab
that brought me strength,
that gave me the resolve
to continue striving
for what I believe in.
Khala Ammi nods and swallows hard.
Her eyes are wide, fully focused,
but her heart is still wavering,
or so I think. . . .

Warning

That same evening
Arsal grabs my new cricket bat
that I tucked behind our mattress.
Before I can wrestle it from him,
he leaves to play in our lane.
Khala Ammi comes into our room
once he is back
and warns Arsal:
Young man, apologize to Aarzu
or you will face severe consequences.
Sure enough, Khala Ammi's warning works;
by night I have a neatly folded sheet of paper
labeled *For Aarzu* waiting on my pillow.
I smirk as I unseal it. . . .

Arsal's Apology

This is just to say
I took your cricket bat
to play
in the street
with the galli boys.

We took turns
spitting on our palms
to get a good grip
on your new bat.

Forgive me, but
what's the point of a bat
when girls can't play
outdoors anyway?

Flying Chappal

When I show Khala Ammi
Arsal's apology,
she yanks her chappal
off her left foot,

                                      balances on her right foot,

and sends her chappal flying,
aimed at Arsal.
He twists his torso,
but not enough.

                >>SPLAT<<

Chappal Mark

a muddy
chappal-print
slaps onto the back
of Arsal's starched
white kameez. And even
though it is going
to be me washing
the dirt off, the warning
he's been given——to never
tease me, or any girl,
again——is worth it!

Apology

Could it be
that I'm the betrayer and Nazia is the betrayed?

Could it be
that Nazia was jealous of all the fun I was having at the bungalow?

Could it be
that Nazia felt she lost a friend when I found a friend in Zoya?

Could it be
that she's now trying to be a better friend?

Could it be
that she's trying to help me in my time of need by buying out all my leftover stock?

Could it be
that I need to apologize to Nazia, instead of her needing to apologize to me?

Game Plan

The next day when Khaloo
leaves to find a buyer for his rickshaw
(since money matters are getting worse),
I tell Khala Ammi of a possible solution
to all the money problems
Khaloo is facing.
She doesn't believe me at first,
but when she accompanies me,
along with Irfan and Sukoon,
to Zoya and Faizan Bhai's home
and witnesses Guard Uncle at the gate
greet me with *Salaam-alaykum, betiya*
and when I tell Zoya and Faizan Bhai
of our dire circumstances—
us needing a home,
Khaloo needing a job—
they immediately understand.
They take Amma into their confidence.
They welcome Khala Ammi
with the same respect they show Amma
and usher us all

to the back of the house
to the lavish servants' quarters.

Match

When Khala Ammi is assured
that we will be able to fund Sukoon's transplant,
the first thing we do is head to the laboratory
to complete the tests
the doctor wrote,
to determine if I am a possible match for Sukoon.
I hope my blood and tissues
do not betray me.

Rent-Free

Unsurprisingly,
the idea of moving to Zoya's house
and living rent-free
is more than welcomed by Khaloo . . .

almost as if he were expecting it.
When Khala Ammi tells Khaloo
that Barai Sahib is in need of a driver
for his new Prado
(a job opportunity Amma and Guard Uncle shared as we left the
    bungalow),
Khaloo nods and almost smiles.
So Khala Ammi bundles it with
the news of my "selection"
to the girls' national cricket team.
Khaloo grunts
his consent?

Moving

Since all our clothes lie in boxes
(because we feared being evicted by our landlord),
it only takes us a couple of hours
the next morning
to pack up our two-bedroom apartment.
Khala Ammi takes me along
to wish our neighbors, *Khuda hafiz*.
She boasts, *You won't miss seeing Aarzu for long.*

She places an arm around my shoulders.
My Aaru has made it to the girls' team.
You'll see her on television now.
As expected, the neighbors *ooh* and *aah*
but not with delight,
rather in contempt.
This time my words
spill out as easily as a breath
that's been held in too long. . . .

They Say   I Say

Too tall for a girl.   *Just right for a cricket player.*

No curves.   *The only curve I care about is the trajectory of the ball that comes toward me as it leaves the bowler's hand.*

It's good she wears a dupatta—it's the only way we can tell she is a girl.   *My dupatta I wear for myself. It isn't a way for others to tell me apart from a boy.*

One Last Task

Twenty minutes before the appointed time
that Faizan Bhai has promised
to have us picked up,
Khala Ammi has an idea.
She rushes to Bano Aunty's house next door.
I assume it is for one last farewell
to her best friend and next-door neighbor.
But Khala Ammi returns, urges Sukoon and I
to bring along the box in which she has packed
kitchen utensils and leftover groceries.
When I see her unbox ingredients at Bano Aunty's—
cardamom, ghee, chickpea flour, and sugar—
I know Khala Ammi is making
a dessert that Mama used to make, baisan ka halva.
She whisks and stirs for fifteen minutes
till the wet mixture clumps like fudge
around her wooden spoon.
A warm, nutty aroma fills the air.
Today isn't Match Day, Khala Ammi, Sukoon reminds her.
I know, Khala Ammi says as she spoons the dessert
into her fanciest glass dish before handing it to me.

This is for your friend Zoya.
Khala Ammi places a hand-embroidered napkin over the halva,
sealing her warmth and gratitude inside.
A tear rolls down her cheek
as her dimple sneaks up.

Leaving Behind

When we're about to leave the apartment,
I turn back and run through the rooms,
checking that we haven't left anything behind.
Arsal catches me mouthing a prayer.

He flicks his hip,
a disdainful thumka-dismissal of the life we lived here
and an attempt to make me laugh.

I smile and hope
the only thing we're leaving behind
is the stench of fried onions
and poverty.

I notice

an Under-15 team list
taped to Zoya's dresser
when I go to give her the
baisan ka halva.

I see our names,
Zoya Sarwar Ejaz,
Aarzu Raza,
right on top.

But I do not see
Tahira's, Zeenat's, Mariam's, Ismat's, or Nazia's name
on the list.

I see a column with each player's city mentioned.
There are girls from
Quetta,
Mansehra,
Gilgit,
Faisalabad,
Lahore,
Islamabad,

Muzaffarabad,
Hyderabad.

Other than Zoya and me,
there are no other girls from Karachi.
I know my seniors, and Nazia, were good.
I wonder if I would've made the team
if Zoya's father hadn't gotten us "selected."

I wonder if none of us girls
made it to the team
on merit
(as the tryout announcement stated).

Zoya is too busy
drooling over the halva
to notice my dismay.

When Sukoon meets Zoya

it is even better than what I imagined.
Sukoooooon! Zoya runs toward Sukoon
and wraps her in a hug

as if she has met a long-lost friend.
Sukoon beams.

Practically purring, Zoya says,
You have two big sisters now!
Not one!
Together we're going to get you well.
#gimme_a_high_five

Dialysis Day

When it's Sukoon's next dialysis day,
I am able to accompany her and Khala Ammi
for the first time ever.
We enter the dialysis unit.
I see people,
young and old,
hooked up to machines.
Wires and tubes
strung and looped
every which way.
I feel weak in my knees
and squeeze Sukoon's hand.

It's okay, Aaru Aapi,
Sukoon says as the nurse prepares her for dialysis.
I take a deep breath,
shut my eyes,
make dua,
and it doesn't even hurt!
I feel hopeful
and fearful
all at once.
I realize,
this is Sukoon's hostile environment
and she has already learned to thrive.

Khaloo at the Bungalow

Khaloo considers the Prado his baby, instead of just being its driver.
> He scrub, scrub, scrubs the tires.
> He wipe, wipe, wipes the windshield.
> He polish, polish, polishes the side mirrors.
> He dust, dust, dusts the seats.
> Then he goes around and around and around it in circles, making sure he hasn't missed a spot to sparkle.

Khaloo considers Barai Sahib, his wife, and kids demigods.
> If he is sitting when they come out of the house, he jumps to his feet.
> If he is standing in their presence, he bows low.
> If they give him instructions, he complies without delay.
> If Barai Sahib has to go somewhere,
> Khaloo is ready by the car an hour or two before.

Khaloo does not huff and puff at Khala Ammi like he used to.
Khala Ammi's cheek no longer turns the color of overripe kishmish.
He even tries to make small talk with me.

I don't know about Khala Ammi,
but I have no regard for Khaloo
or his change in behavior.

Some
wounds
are
too
deep
to
heal.

Back at School

When I try to make eye contact
with Nazia during school,
she stares at her shoes instead.

She shows no interest in cricket,
doesn't turn in her assignments,
and leaves school before I can catch up with her.

Words of Wisdom

When I tell Khala Ammi
about Nazia's odd behavior
as she embroiders a pouch
(as a token of gratitude for Amma),
she holds up her embroidery and smiles.
Friendships are like this, Aaru.
I squint at the neat, five-petaled flower she has cross-stitched.
What? I don't get it, I say impatiently.
Just tell me why I can't have my best friend back.
Khala Ammi flips the cloth around.

Stray threads crisscross and tangle.

Notice these knots.
They're an inconvenience;
my threads tangle in them often,
but they hold everything in place.
And it's only when I work through the issues at the back
that the surface pattern blooms.
These knots are like complicated situations
that you need to work through.

But Nazia isn't doing any of the work!
Friendship is a two-way street! I retort.

Ahaan. Put yourself in her shoes, Aaru.
She showed you the ropes when you were new here.
Think how she must've felt losing you to Zoya!
And to top it all off, you've moved into Zoya's house.
How do you think she feels now?

Make Amends!

Nazia wasn't at fault
for telling Khala Ammi
where to find me.
She didn't even tell on me,
like I initially thought.

She probably thought
I'd found a new best friend,
in all the stories I shared about the bungalow.
And that must've made her jealous
and mad,
and that's probably why
she was so cold
and distant.

Zoya is a good friend.
But I miss Nazia,
and who said I can't keep both?

Hiccups

After a couple of weeks of practice
    with the coach at Zoya's,
    with my seniors at school,
    with the new team at a cricket academy,
everything is finally lined up—
our Under-15 girls cricket team
is set to play our first match against
some of Pakistan's favorite retired male players.
We hope to attract
lots of attention to the game, but . . .
trouble brews.
We attract attention all right,
but not from where we expect it.
The so-called Islamic clergy and death threats
come knocking at the doors of the bungalow
the morning of the scheduled match.
They make it clear.
These girls cannot play against these men, they say.
They are our national heroes.
What if the men lose?
We cannot have men lose to girls!

On the Field

When I bat, when I bowl,
I'm forever on a roll.

Cricket field
is my shield.
Not concealed,
will not yield.

This is my sport.
Ball's in my court.
Easy retort,
won't come up short.

When I bat, when I bowl,
I'm forever on a roll.

Across the Line

As in a risky shot that is highly rewarding if timed correctly.
As in the solution I suggest so we can continue with our game.

If girls play girls,
we can at least have a match!
We don't have to play veterans.
We don't have to play men at all!

Change in Strategy

It is a risk,
but one we'll have to take.
The change in strategy means
we need another squad of girl players
to form another team
that we can play against.
And although it may be a challenge
to convince the girls and their families
from our locality,

Zoya and I decide to knock at every door
to invite girls from our neighborhood to play
on the team.
I know Mariam, Tahira, Zeenat, and Ismat
would love to join.
But we need more players to sign up.
We take along our spare uniforms
in hopes that the fame will lure them in.
Guards from Barai Sahib's army of servants
accompany us,
ensuring security.

When I Was Little

Every year when the summer sun
baked our peaches golden-orange,
Baba would place a ladder
against the trunk of our peach tree
and declare it was time to harvest.

And every year
I would hesitate about

climbing to the top.
I'd offer to stay down
with the basket
to catch the peaches.
I'd tell Baba to go up instead.

But Baba would remind me,
It's only hard the first few rungs.
You know the reward will be sweet
and worth the effort.

I'd scratch the back of my left leg
with the tip of my right foot,
clutch on to the sides of the ladder,
and climb,
rung by rung,
one
two
three
fasterandfaster.

Rung by rung,
I'd leave my fears behind
till the fragrance of the peaches

enveloped me in a warm embrace
celebrating my feat.

My dream of playing

in a jersey my size,
with gold-lettered
Aarzu Raza
flashing in defiance
at all those who mocked me
is slowly coming true.
I'm climbing the ladder
rung by rung,
leaving my fears
(of what Khaloo and the neighbors will say)
behind.
I'm helping other girls
do the same.
After the first few
slow sign-ups,
the going gets easier.
More and more girls join,

and lead us to their friends' houses.
Our team of girls grows
fasterandfaster
until we are more than enough girls
to form two whole teams.
This game is ON!

One More

We break from knocking on doors to cool off with Pakola sodas.
We have enough, more than enough girls, Zoya declares,
tapping the tips of her emerald-painted fingernails against each other.
Time to get everyone some uniforms!
                  Not yet, I say, taking one last chug of my soda.
                         There's one more house
                            I need to visit.
                     I've been saving the best for last.

Crossroad or Crossword?

         N A Z I A
             A
             R
         Z O Y A
             U

Who said I can't have two best friends?

I can be the one
who apologizes to Nazia.
I can be the one
who invites Nazia to join the team.
I can be the one
who makes up to Nazia by sharing my new friend.
I can be the one
who introduces Zoya to Nazia.
I can be the one
who introduces Nazia to Zoya.

Make Up

When Nazia opens her door
and sees me,
her eyebrows reach for her hairline
in disbelief.
I lean in close
so only she can hear.

I'm sorry, I whisper.

And?

Thank you for giving me the courage to take the job at the bungalow.

And?

You were right? I give her my thousand-watt smile.

Nazia's lips slowly curl up at the corners.
Better late than never!
Nazia says in her *I-told-you-so* Nazia tone.
Then she throws her arms around me,
engulfing me in a back-popping hug.
And all the awkwardness between us melts away
like a kulfi in the summer sun.

Like Old Times, but Better

Nazia kicks a pebble.
It lands a few steps ahead of me.
                                               Zoya looks confused.
                   I pull her in.
Nazia steps back.
                I interlock elbows
                  with them both,
        one on either   side of me.
                Nazia, Aarzu, Zoya.
           A skip, a hop, and a jump forward.
                I kick the pebble next.
Skip.
                      Hop.
                                            Jump.
                                 Zoya catches on,
                        kicks the pebble forward.
               Skip.
               Hop.
               Jump.
             And a leap
             to new friendships.

A Perfect Match

When my blood and tissue results
finally come in,
it is news as sweet as jalebis.
The doctor tells us
more tests will follow,
but the most important results are already in.
I am a perfect match for Sukoon.
Alhamdulillah, Shukr Alhamdulillah.
Gratitude spreads over me
like ghee on hot parathas.
MamaBaba's words come to mind.
They add the perfect honey drizzle—
Being grateful for blessings
brings more blessings.
I pray that my gratitude
brings more opportunities
for me to be grateful. . . .
I pray that our first cricket match is
a perfect match too.

Tune In

Khala Ammi is the most excited
when we have a date for the match.
Since this is the first match,
and it's only girls competing,
it won't get coverage
on national television.

But that doesn't stop Khala Ammi
from taking Irfan along
to inform everyone and their dogs
(if they have any)
to tune in to the commentary on their radios.

When Irfan returns
from our old neighborhood,
he grabs one of my dupattas,
impersonating Khala Ammi,
and knock, knock, knocks
at all the windows and doors
in the servants' quarter,
makes his voice shrill, and says,

Three days from today
tune in to your radios at five p.m.
Channel FM 91.
My Aaru is on the girl's cricket team. . . .
My Aaru . . .
My Aaru!
Sukoon holds her sides and giggles.
Khala Ammi blushes.
It wasn't exactly like that!
And I throw my arms around her
and hug her like never before.

Payback Time

Khala Ammi finds out
that Arsal used the money
from my bat-doodled gullak
to buy brand-new cricket gear
for himself
and his galli boys.
She makes him retrieve every piece:
Cricket bats.

Cricket balls.
Helmets.
Wicketkeeping gloves.
Wicketkeeping pads.
Batting gloves.
Protective pads.
Cricket shoes.
Cricket bags.
She makes him wipe them down
till they shine.
She instructs him
to present them to me
to share with my friends.

Our Match Day

I am on strike.
Shins shuffle.
Brain buffers.
Pads adjust.
Bat strikes.
Arms sweep.

Dupatta flutters.
Grin grows.
Fielder ducks.
Heart hammers.
Heads tilt.
Eyes squint.
Boundaries shrink.
Hands rise.
Umpire signals.
Applause echoes.
Team cheers.
Kulfis melt.
Pakola bottles clink.
ChaKKA! It's a SIX.

Stained Hands

My hands
stained red
the color of love
from the cork ball.

My hands
stained white
the color of peace
from chalk paint on the crease.

My hands
stained brown
the color of my skin
from dust off the field
tell a story of a dream realized.

New Innings

My ears tune in to Sukoon's and Arsal's voices
shrieking, *Aaru Aapi, Aaru Aapi*
above the cheering crowds.
I hold my hands up,
palms facing the skies,
wet with tears,
then
f
    a
        l
           l
                to the ground in prostration.

Nazia and Zoya flank me on either side.
Our foreheads touch the earth together in sujood.
Our hands press flat together against the pitch.
They join me in thanking Allah.

Alhamdulillah!

GLOSSARY

AATA: whole wheat flour, also referred to kneaded dough made from whole wheat flour

ACHAAR: pickled vegetables and raw mango soaked in oil or vinegar, doused in spicy masala, and fermented in the sun, eaten as a side dish

ADHĀN: Muslim call to prayer

ALHAMDULILLAH: "praise be to Allah," a common phrase of gratitude

ALOO: potato

AYE HAYE: "Oh no!"—phrase to express disappointment

BAILAN: rolling pin

BAINGAN RAITA: eggplant yogurt

BAISAN KA HALVA: fudge-like dessert made of chickpea flour, sugar, ghee, and cardamom

BASANT: spring kite-flying festival celebrated in South Asia

BIRISTA: fried onions

BIRYANI: spiced rice dish containing meat and saffron-flavored rice

BISMILLAH: "with the name of Allah," an Arabic phrase at the start of most chapters of the Qur'an, also used by Muslims when they start anything new

BOTI: chunk of meat

CHAADAR: huge piece of cloth draped over a woman's clothing
CHALO: "let's go"
CHAPPAL: slipper
CHARPOYS: hand-woven, foldable beds
CHHAKKA: sixer/six runs—when the batswoman/batsman plays a shot that does not bounce before it reaches the boundary
CHOTAI SAHIB: "young master"
CHUTNEY: sweet and tangy dipping sauce made with tamarind pulp, mint leaves, and brown sugar
DAAL CHAWAL: ground lentil gravy and rice
DAIGHCHI: small pot
DHABA: roadside café
DUA: short personalized or standard Muslim prayer, usually made by raising hands to the heavens
DUM KA KEEMA: smoked mincemeat dish
DUPATTA: piece of cloth, usually worn on the head or draped over the chest—part of Pakistani women's national dress
FAJR: Muslim pre-sunrise prayer
GALLI: narrow street or alleyway often found in residential areas
GARAM MASALA: blend of spices—including cinnamon, peppercorns, cardamom, mustard seeds, coriander seeds, cloves, mace, and nutmeg—used whole or in powdered form
GATHRI: bundle
GHEE: clarified butter
GOL TAKIYA: log-shaped pillow

GOTI: playing piece (token) used in board games

GULLAK: sealed clay money container (without a lid) that needs to be smashed with a hammer to retrieve the savings

GUPSHUP: chitchat

HIJAB: head-covering worn by Muslim women

INSHALLAH: "if Allah wills," a common phrase used by Muslims when talking about an event that they hope will happen in the future

JALEBI: deep-fried, sweet snack made of a flour-based batter dipped in sweet syrup

JAO: go

JEE: yes

JHARO: long broom that is used to sweep the floor from a squatting position

KACHUMBAR: grated or finely chopped vegetables served with or without yogurt as a side dish or condiment

KAMEEZ: traditional Pakistani shirt worn by men and women

KARAK CHAI: strong cup of milk tea

KHALA AMMI: "aunt mom"—maternal aunt

KHALOO: maternal uncle

KHUDA HAFIZ: "may God protect you," a common phrase for farewell in Muslim societies

KIA: what

KISHMISH: raisins

KORMA: thick gravy dish with braised meat, yogurt, and vegetables

KULFI: popular South Asian milk-based ice cream on a stick flavored with saffron, cardamom, pistachio, and almonds, served chilled
LARKI: girl
LASSI: sweet or salty yogurt drink
LUDO: game for two to six players who throw dice to advance their tokens around a board
MAGHRIB AND ISHA: nighttime Muslim prayers
MANGAL BAZAAR: weekly Tuesday market
MASJID: mosque
NAFSIYATI: psychotic, insane
PAKORAS: fried fritters made of onion, potatoes, chickpea flour, and spices
PALLOS: long sides of a dupatta
PARATHAS: flaky flatbread, often fried in ghee
RICKSHAW: three-wheeled open cab, a common form of public transport in Asia
ROTI: flatbread rolled out and cooked on a pan on a stove
RUKHSATI: farewell ceremony in Pakistani culture for the bride when she leaves for the groom's house
SABZI: vegetables, cooked or uncooked
SAHIB: master
SAJDAH: single act of prostration
SALAH: Muslim prayer
SALAM-ALAIYKUM: "peace be upon you," a Muslim greeting

SAMAJHDAR: sensible

SAMOSA: fried, stuffed snack that has a crispy layered outer casing with mashed vegetables or meat inside

SHAHI TUKRAY: fried slices of bread soaked in sweetened saffron milk

SHALWAR: traditional Pakistani baggy trousers worn by men and women

SHAMI KEBAB: meat-based kebab

SHARBAT: cold beverage made by mixing a flavored, concentrated sugar syrup with cold water or milk

SHUKR ALHAMDULILLAH: phrase showing gratefulness and praise to Allah for His blessings

SUJOOD: prostration, one of the main pillars of daily prayer in Islam

TAJ: crown

TANDOOR NAAN: flatbread baked in a kiln oven

TANDOOR WALA: person/place where you get tandoor flatbread

TASBIH: prayer beads used by Muslims

TAWA: large flat griddle or frying pan used to make flatbreads like roti

THELLA: hand-pulled cart or trolley carrying produce, street food, or goods to be sold

THUMKA: subcontinent dance move that involves a flick of the hips

TIJORI: metal chest that can be locked, commonly used for safekeeping in South Asia

TOTKA: home remedy
ZABARDAST: bravo
ZUHR AND ASR: daytime Muslim prayers

TYPES OF POETRY IN THIS BOOK

ACROSTIC POEM: a poem where the first letters of each line spells out a word or phrase, like in the poem "Zoya"

ANAPHORA POEM: a poetic technique in which successive lines begin with the same phrase, like in the poem "I Want to Tell Khala Ammi"

BLACKOUT POEM: a form of poetry where words from a larger text are blackened out to leave words that form a new poem with a completely different meaning from the original text, like the graffiti on the wall in the poem "Selected"

CONCRETE POEM: also known as a "shape" poem, conveys art and verse at the same time; the words are formatted in a way to enhance the meaning and visual imagery of the words, like the poems "Khaloo," "Arsal," "Khala Ammi," "Irfan," and "Gol Rotis"

FALSE APOLOGY POEM: These poems are inspired by William Carlos Williams. In a false apology poem the person apologizing feels compelled to say sorry, in spite of their lack of sympathy. "This is just to say" is usually the first line, and "forgive me" can be added in the last stanza of the poem, like in the poem "Arsal's Apology."

FREE VERSE: poetry that does not rhyme or have a regular rhythm

GHAZAL: This is a Middle Eastern and subcontinental form of poetry that is composed of five to fifteen couplets. Each line of the poem must be of the same length. The first couplet introduces a scheme, made up of a rhyme followed by a refrain. Subsequent couplets repeat the refrain and rhyme the second line with both lines of the first stanza. The final couplet usually includes the poet's signature, referring to the author in the first or third person.[1] For an example, see the poem "#Napkin_Ghazal."

LEARN MORE ABOUT POETIC FORMS HERE: writersdigest.com/write-better-poetry/list-of-50-poetic-forms-for-poets

---

[1] "Ghazal", Poets.org, accessed October 1, 2024, poets.org/glossary/ghazal.

KHALA AMMI'S SHAHI TUKRAY RECIPE

(Only try this recipe with a parent or guardian)

INGREDIENTS

oil or ghee for frying

5 slices of bread cut into triangles

1 quart of milk

1 pinch of saffron strands

5 tablespoons of sugar

1 teaspoon of cardamom powder

optional: pistachios, almonds, and cashew nuts for sprinkling

METHOD

1. Heat ghee or oil in a pan and deep-fry the bread triangles on medium-low flame till they turn golden brown.
2. In a pot, boil the milk with saffron strands, sugar, and cardamom powder. Leave the milk mixture to cook on a low flame until it reduces to one third its original amount.
3. Now dip the fried bread slices into the reduced milk mixture until the liquid has been soaked up.
4. Garnish with chopped nuts.

AUTHOR'S NOTE

AARZU'S STORY IS ONE INSPIRED BY TRUE EVENTS.

I was surrounded by some of the most supportive men growing up, and I consider myself lucky. I've heard and seen, firsthand, the discrimination against girls for as long as I can remember. When I was Aarzu's age, it broke my heart to see the maternity ward nurse at the hospital at which my third sister was born refuse to show my mother her baby. They whisked the baby away to another room without revealing her gender. When my mother kept asking to see her baby, they took my nani, my grandmother, aside and told her that her daughter had given birth to a fourth girl. My grandmother was overjoyed and went to congratulate my mother and ordered sweets to be distributed at the hospital. The nurses and doctors were in shock. Later they informed us that they had had cases of mothers who fell prey to depression because of the societal pressure on women to produce a male offspring.

Like Aarzu's, my craze for cricket was intense during my tween and teen years. I remember lurking around the door of my apartment in Karachi, Pakistan, when I was thirteen, hoping to get a chance to play cricket in the corridors of our building. But every time, I heard the same reply from boys younger and older than me. "No! You are a girl!" they would remind me matter-of-factly, as if that were explanation enough.

Aarzu's transformation to Azlan was inspired by the story of Maria Toorpakai Wazir, Pakistan's star squash player whose father disguised her as a boy, going as far as changing her name to Genghis Khan to hide her from the Taliban invaders in northern Pakistan while allowing her to pursue her passion for squash.

The resolution of this story is inspired by Shaiza and Sharmeen Khan, known as "the Khan Sisters," who in 1993 were the real-life pioneers of women's cricket in Pakistan. The newly formed team faced a fate similar to Aarzu and Zoya's when they set up a preliminary match against the former men's cricket team in Karachi. In an interview, Shaiza, the older of the two sisters, said, "The fundamentalists, they did not agree with what we were doing. They thought it was un-Islamic. And it was in all [the] newspapers that they were going to storm my house. So, my father [a rich carpet merchant of Karachi], said you better call off this game. And you better play it between two women's sides, which we did."[2]

I pray this story brings hope and reminds young girls everywhere that they are indeed stronger than they think.

---

2   Arfath Pasha S, "Sisters who broke boundaries for women's cricket in Pakistan", *Crick Tracker*, May 17, 2024, crictracker.com/cricket-opinion/sisters-who-broke-boundaries-for-womens-cricket-in-pakistan.

ACKNOWLEDGMENTS

ALHAMDULILLAH TIMES INFINITY! I'M SO GRATEFUL TO ALLAH (SWT) for His countless blessings and the inspiration, faith, and strength that I've discovered, and continue to discover, through His Mercy, in the words of the Qur'an. I never dreamed my humble Qur'an journaling efforts in 2019 (with my then two- and nine-year-old kids) would lead me to writing faith-inspired letters (like Aarzu's) to my own kids, which would morph into books and allow me to share stories of hope and faith with kids worldwide someday.

I'm also incredibly grateful to:

My dada, Aziz Dharamsey, who lives in my heart and prayers even though I never got to meet him. Like Sukoon, my dada suffered from kidney disease, but unlike Sukoon, he couldn't get the medical help he required and passed away when my dad, my abu, was only two years old.

My dadi (Tahira), nani (Mariam), mama (Ismat), and khala (Zeenat), who inspired the names of Aarzu's friends in the book, have been the most inspiring women in my life—Dadi, for being the best roommate through my teen years. Nani, for showing me how to focus on the reverse of the embroidery piece (like Aarzu's khala showed her) and always giving up her favorite rocking chair spot by her bookshelf while allowing me to indulge in her stacks of prized books and *Reader's Digests*. Mama, for always making the best rotis (round or not) and for teaching us there's so much more to life than gol rotis! Khala, for being my second mom and the best aunt ever!

Nazia Khan, my backbone through university and the needle to my compass of life (sorry for being sappy, but it's true). You don't know how much our friendship means to me.

Irfan, my younger cousin IRL and childhood partner in crime, thank you for all the priceless memories at 08 Amir Khusro Road, Karachi, Pakistan!

Dr. Sahr Syed, my cheerleader and friend, and her daughter, Safa, who buy, read, love, and recommend every book I have written and make sure to share them with friends far and wide! I have no words for how happy each voice note, message, and picture of my books (front-facing) on your library shelves makes me.

Dr. Areeba Jawed—MD, FASN, assistant professor, Division of Nephrology, University of Michigan, a.k.a my trusty Josephian school friend—for helping me get all the medical facts right and graciously answering all my questions at any time of day or night.

My sisters, Raazieh, Aliya, and Zehra, for making dua for me, hearing me whine, and consoling me through all my literary endeavors.

Abu, my dad, for always being supportive, encouraging, and for proudly announcing all my successes to extended family WhatsApp groups (which is always embarrassing in the moment, but feels good later).

Abbas, my husband, for double-checking all the cricket-related information in this book, entertaining me with memes when things got serious, and being patient as I endlessly revised and edited this debut novel.

Chaaya Prabhat, for the gorgeous cover and all the fun doodles inside.

The visionary poets of the subcontinent, Mir Taqi Mir, Muhammad Iqbal, Faiz Ahmed Faiz, and Mirza Ghalib, whose ghazals, marsiyas, and nazms have inspired me since childhood.

Agent Lynnette Novak, who is sweet, supportive, and settles for nothing but the best! This book has had quite a journey prepublication, and I couldn't have done it without her believing in my passion, answering all my big and small questions, probing me to dig deeper to fully explore the GMCs for Aarzu's story, calming my nerves, and continuing to be the best companion on this crazy publishing journey.

Editor Krista Vitola, who fell in love with Aarzu and Sukoon and signed off her first correspondence with me with the words "your fan." Your editorial notes set off light bulbs in my brain, and I was able to clearly foreshadow and connect the dots as I revised.

Renee LaTulippe, for her lyrical language tutorials and her LLL course that have taught me so much.

Fellow authors and friends: Janet Wong, Kwame Alexander, Nikki Grimes, Reem Faruqi, Laura Shovan, Lisa Fipps, Thanhha Lai, and Jasmin Warga, for their inspiring novels in verse and poetry collections that served as great mentor texts as I wrote this novel. A special shout-out to Kirsten W. Lawrson, Zainab Hassan, Shondra, Maryam Shahjani, Batool Ali, and Kari Gonzales for reading the very first draft and offering their suggestions and support along the way.

Author Shirin (Aunty) Shamsi, for being the first to tell me to write fearlessly about my culture and religion.

To everyone at Simon & Schuster, my village who helped bring my book to life: Deeba Zargarpur, Morgan York, Alin Haberle, Laura Eckes, Palavi Ahuja, Maryam Ahmad, and Bara MacNeil.

The Writing Barn and the Highlights Foundation for their scholarships; learning the ropes of drafting a middle-grade novel from Rajani LaRocca was a treat. Cordelia Jensen's Novel in Verse course with helpful prompts showed me how playful we can be in both content and form, and many of my favorite poems were drafted during the course.

ABOUT THE AUTHOR

MARZIEH IS A BAKER TURNED AWARD-WINNING AUTHOR. SHE loves adding magic to her creations—whether that's a seven-layered rainbow cake or the books she writes for children all over the world. Her work is inspired by her Pakistani culture and Muslim heritage. As a teenager, Marzieh used to love watching cricket, but following heartbreak from Pakistan's 1999 Cricket World Cup loss, she stopped watching the game altogether.

Marzieh enjoys learning new skills, jumping rope, sipping chai, and observing nature. Marzieh dreams of owning a talking parrot someday. But until then she lives in Pakistan with her husband and children, who inspire her daily.